The Other Lovecraft

BY KYLE PAQUET

Text and cover art copyright © 2011 Kyle Paquet. All rights reserved.

978-0-557-59823-6

For Jessica, who is the reason this was written in the first place.

You'll always be my inspiration, Jess.

There has long been a very distinctive line between fiction and reality. The definition thereof is found in humankind's specific understanding of what can be observed in the practical, tangible world, and what is simply unreal and extraordinary.

This being the case, how would you react if I were to say, "Upon a rooftop on this dank October night, two beings of unearthly countenance sat watching"?

You will no doubt discard this as fantastical fiction, and insist (somewhat ignorantly) there is no such thing as the Elder Race, but I assure you that I pen this work in total earnest. Well, maybe not quite total earnest, more like *mostly* earnest.

Like, if you measured this book on an earnestness scale of one to ten, and ten is like really true, and one is really not true, it's probably around a four point five.

Again, you may dismiss this text as insane drivel, and could not possibly have happened in a sane, logical world.

In that respect, dear reader, I agree with you wholeheartedly.

I

In Which the Main Protagonists are Introduced

==

CITY OF ARKHAM, MASSACHUSETTS, OCTOBER 10

Upon a rooftop on a dank October night, two beings of unearthly countenance sat watching. In physical appearance they were most alien; abnormally tall, possessing greenish-black skin, clawed hands, and large, leathery wings that folded neatly beneath the heavy, flowing coats they wore. Their faces, partially hidden behind plain surgical masks, may almost have looked human, but for the odd shape of the head and the bundle of tentacles sprouting from the mouth.

The two were of an ancient race, one that has operated amongst humans undetected for hundreds of generations.

They were Cthulhi, and they were the nomad warriors of the doomed world of R'lyeh.

A brooding silence had fallen between the two, as the younger, who stood close to the ledge, had no fondness for the task at hand.

"I am still not sure that I understand all of this," he growled in his native tongue.

The Elder stood from where he crouched in a shadowy corner, approached the young Cthulhi as he observed the alley below.

"This has been explained to you, E'nasa," the Elder explained, "We need an agent to live amongst the human beings, learn their ways, become like them."

"I know this, Elder Dagot," E'nasa sighed, "what I don't understand is the necessity for this particular individual to be... a *girl*."

In the alley below, the dim, flickering light revealed a woman that looked to be just into her twenties, sporting short black hair and green eyes that seemed to glow with unearthly ether. Attractive by human standards, her athletic figure was explained in part by her current activities; which apparently called for the use of a submachine gun, a double-barrelled shotgun, and a rather large katana. E'nasa unconsciously glanced at the moderately-sized, crescent-shaped sword strapped to his own back and felt oddly meek.

"I'm not good with girls."

"This particular girl single-handedly wiped out a Shoggoth infestation in Kingsport, and the Mi-Go invasion right here in Arkham."

The girl appeared to be tracking something. She stooped to examine a seemingly bare patch of ground.

"It is impressive, so be sure," E'nasa said. "But there must be far more suitable candidates than I."

The girl looked up, stared straight at the watching Cthulhi.

"On the contrary, E'nasa," Dagot said sardonically. "You may consider yourself versed in the ways of combat, but you have much to learn of the world in which you dwell. Anyway, Asenath here seems just your type. Also, I've already set up a meeting."

E'nasa looked from the alley to Elder Dagot, reverently stating, "I hate you."

DID YOU KNOW?!?!?

The Cthulhi and the Mi-Go have been at war for nine and a half centuries. Halfway into the war, the Mi-Go captured and conquered the Cthulhi's home-world of Rl'yeh. Since then several hundred campaigns have been made to try and retake Rl'yeh, but all have ended in stark disaster.

E'nasa, along with a great number of other Cthulhi, were not born on Rl'yeh, and have unfortunately never even seen their home-world.

II

In Which Both Coffee and Awkward Moments are Shared

==

THRESHOLD ISLAND, PENNSYLVANIA OCTOBER 12

Grounded!™ Coffee House was located on the corner of Jackson and Chesterfield in downtown Threshold. It was a relatively shabby establishment, despite the fact that it belonged to a fairly large chain.

The table that E'nasa currently sat at was an evil and gaudy yellow, scratched and leaning 5 degrees to the (relative) left. E'nasa looked over the double espresso he held, at Asenath, who was simply staring at E'nasa with smug fascination. Up close, she was even more attractive, in spite of her heavily-shadowed eyes and messy hair. He sat the espresso down, wondering why he even bothered ordering it, as removing his mask would be incredibly taboo.

"So," E'nasa finally broke the ice. "You name has... Asenath White?"

"Yes, but everybody calls me Natty," she replied. "And your English is terrible."

"I sorry. I know English word, but not used to speak English. Nether thought good idea to try."

"Why not?"

E'nasa looked embarrassedly to his left. He happened to glance the small boy of about six who was staring at him with wide eyes. A simple growl was enough to dismiss the boy.

"You don't like kids?" Natty asked.

E'nasa shook his head, "Not."

"Not what?"

"Not like kids. They small."

"Yeah, I noticed."

Natty took a sip of her black coffee.

"So," she said. "I never caught your name."

E'nasa cocked his head.

"Don't know. Probably can't say."

"Try me."

"It's E'nasa," he said, pronouncing the name in his native accent.

"'Snsnasosa'?" Natty replied, stumbling over the unfamiliar syllables.

"No, 'E'nasa.'"

"'Linolonaso'?"

"No, it's..." he started, but then finished. "Just calls 'Cthulhu'."

"Cthulhu," Natty half-smiled. "I like that."

"Good."

A silence fell between them, which consisted of Natty sipping her coffee while she watched E'nasa/Cthulhu watching her sip her coffee. Needless to say, it was quite awkward for both of them, but perhaps mildly interesting to any passers-by.

It was Natty that broke the silence this time by saying, "So, Cthulhu, what's your next move?"

"Move?" Cthulhu said. "Did not think 'bout that."

He thought a bit more, then said, "I guess I need place for to sleep."

"You sleep?"

"Is that problem?"

"No, not really. Just a little unexpected. But it's gonna be almost impossible to find a place in Threshold this time of year."

"So, what do you think to do?"

"Well," she said. "You could stay at my place."

It took a moment for Cthulhu to realize that he had crushed the espresso in his hand, sending hot liquid splashing onto the table. Natty suppressed a laugh.

"You think that good idea?"

"Why not? You're here to study me, right?"

"I not want to study *that* close..."

Natty cocked an eyebrow. "Are you blushing?"

"Uh... no," Cthulhu said defensively.

Natty smiled. "I think you're blushing."

"Cthulhi do not blush."

"Then why did your face turn greener?"

"I has an allergies."

"Right. So what do you say?"

"To stay at you place?"

"Yeah."

"Well," Cthulhu said with a sigh. "I guess I has no choose."

DID YOU KNOW?!?!?

Cthulhi do not get allergies. In fact, they are immune to all human ailments, with the exceptions of tuberculosis, scurvy, the common cold, and hiccups. They do, however, blush.

III

In Which Cthulhu Faces the Horrors of Natty's Apartment

==

THRESHOLD ISLAND, LATER

Even though Cthulhu had a thorough knowledge of English terms, he couldn't (or quite possibly did not wish to) grasp Natty's meaning of "apartment." He understood it to be a dwelling of some kind, but he couldn't picture living within these huge, vertical buildings. As a naturally space-faring entity, the thought of living in such an enclosed domicile made him nauseous.

"How are you doing there, Cthulhu?"

He could think of no way to verbally express his anxiety about the strange building to his new caretaker, so he curled his four fingers in, left his thumb up; a gesture Natty had taught him, meaning "everything is good." He found human gestures intriguing.

Suddenly, Cthulhu noticed that Natty had moved ahead, toward the entrance to the building, while he himself remained rooted firmly to the curb.

For some reason, he couldn't move.

"Something wrong, Cthulhu?"

He shook his head.

He wanted to move. He really did. But somehow, after all of the Mi-Go he had killed without hesitation, all of the battles he had fought without reserve, this strange building had managed to evoke an unfamiliar reaction.

He was terrified.

"Cthulhu...?"

Alright, thought the Cthulhi. *Time to move.*

He managed to gain enough strength to shuffle to the entrance, which was a strange, revolving device that terrified Cthulhu even more than the building itself.

"What on earth is wrong, Cthulhu? It's a revolving door," said Natty irritably, lowering her voice to add, "you've hunted aliens all your life and you're afraid of a door?"

Normally, Cthulhu would've delighted in putting his blade through her skull. But he had orders: no killing humans. Especially this one, as she was one of the few who were proactive in their role in this war.

"Are you coming, or what?" She preceded him through the ominously blade-like spinning door.

Cthulhu nodded, then eyed the revolving portal of doom once more.

Squeezing his eyes shut, he stepped through, keeping his feet moving in short strides as he'd seen others doing before him.

When he opened his eyes once more, he was in a large room with a shining marble floor.

This wasn't so bad.

==

Cthulhu felt certain that he was going to die.

He was trapped in a small box with thin, beige-coloured walls. All he knew was that they were going up, and with every blink of the lights above the unopening door, he felt closer to his impending doom. It wasn't until he saw Natty cringe that he noticed that he was crushing her hand. He hadn't even realized he'd been holding it.

He quickly released her hand, and she immediately began to massage it. It was very possible he had just broken it. He looked at her with sympathy, which she somehow registered.

"It's okay," She said, the pain showing in her voice.

She looked up, saw that the light now rested on

"4." The doors opened, and Cthulhu felt he could breathe again.

"Let's go put some ice on this, shall we?"

She took Cthulhu's hand in her undamaged one (Cthulhu slightly recoiled at the action) and led him out of the elevator into the hallway. After walking down the tight, white-and-red wallpapered hallway, Natty and Cthulhu reached another—albeit smaller—portal. This one was brown, made of wood—a strange, coarse material that Cthulhu was not very familiar with. It was adorned with a metal plate that bore the numerals "428." Using her good hand, Natty removed a small keychain from her pocket, which housed only a few keys. She selected one, put it in the lock, turned it, and the door opened. Inside, the room was smallish, but large for a common apartment. Everything was decorated in shades of dark blue, and smelled of fresh leather.

Strangely, the place reminded Cthulhu of home...

"I'm not here much," said Natty, heading to the kitchen. "I travel a lot for work."

Cthulhu growled in understanding.

"I guess that's why you guys picked me."

Cthulhu suddenly realized that he wasn't in public, and that he was having a bit of trouble breathing. He removed his mask and trench coat, stretching his cooped-up wings. The room was warm.

Natty returned from the kitchen, holding a bag of

ice against her hand. She was trying to wrap a bandage around the bag, to secure it to her throbbing hand.

Seeing as she wasn't having an easy time of it, Cthulhu took the bandage, began to wrap it around Natty's hand himself. Natty found him to be surprisingly gentle. Cthulhu couldn't help noticing the deep green of her eyes.

The girl caught herself looking into the Star-Spawn's eyes, thinking of his gentle demeanour now, and his irrational, comical fear of the revolving doors and the elevator earlier. She suddenly looked away, her pale cheeks flushing with embarrassment.

Cthulhu turned slightly greener.

Natty took her hand away, massaged it.

"Thanks."

Cthulhu croaked a "You're welcome" in his native tongue, and Natty nodded.

What's the matter with me? Thought the Cthulhi.

DID YOU KNOW?!?!?

The Cthulhi do not use any form of processed, artificial, or directed energy (such as electricity). Rather, they have developed all their technology to run off of their own ambient bioelectricity. When a Cthulhi is in close proximity to a Cthulhi-made device, the device will activate. Some require actual physical contact to be made. Furthermore, Cthulhi dwellings are lit by wall-mounted, energy-reactive plates that run on even fainter traces of bioelectricity than other, more complex devices.

IV

In Which Cthulhu Roams Threshold.

==

THRESHOLD ISLAND, OCTOBER 29

The thing coiled in front of Cthulhu like some demented, obscene snake. It was long and serpentine, topped with a chrome-coloured head. It hissed in Cthulhu's face as if to mock him, spat a stream of hot liquid into his right eye. Cthulhu roared...

...and threw down the spray head, growling angrily.

Natty had been doing most of the dishes after breakfast, so Cthulhu had decided to help. He knew the gist of it, putting the water and the cleaning agent into the sink, wiping the dishes with the cloth...

What he couldn't master was this confounded sprayer. Despite the fact that his race hailed from a planet of eighty-percent water, no matter what way he pointed the thing, it always managed to drench him.

He told himself that there was no way this thing would conquer him, but rationalized that he'd never been to his home planet, and therefore, perhaps water-driven entities were a particular point of weakness for him.

Natty just managed to confine a chuckle to a slight snicker.

Cthulhu glared at her, growled in frustration.

Natty correctly interpreted his alien expression (she'd gotten rather good at it).

"It's alright, Cthulhu. Nobody's good with dishes."

She spoke the words, but Cthulhu noticed that her amused expression didn't waver. Instead of getting angry with his handler, Cthulhu simply once more scooped up the sprayer, wheezed and growled a stream of Elder-Tongue curses at it, and once more threw it into the sink.

"Piece of plank," Cthulhu said in his own, flawed version of English.

"Crap," corrected Natty. "Piece of crap."

Cthulhu looked at her, looked at the sprayer. At her again. Considered spraying her with the device, but could only see that course of action ending badly for him.

"Yes. Crap," he said finally.

"Better."

She suddenly looked to her watch, realized the time was indeed 8:45 AM.

"Oh, man, I gotta go."

She turned to leave, and the large Cthulhi trailed behind her.

"Go? Where?"

"Work, Cthulhu. Remember? I got that job at the bank."

She was in a hurry, and she rushed to the door as she flung her coat over her shoulders.

"What... What I do?"

"I dunno. But you've got the keys. You can go out if you want, but you'll have to keep a low profile."

Cthulhu nodded in understanding; stealth was one of the things he knew best.

"Just remember your English and you should be fine."

Before Cthulhu could say another word, Natty was already out the door and gone.

Cthulhu stood there, in the middle of the room, for a long while. Finally, his eyes found the far wall, where hung his coat and mask.

Why not?

==

Cthulhu walked along the crowded street, his disguise now in place. People bustled about their various tasks, and Cthulhu took interest in the fact that everyone seemed to be going somewhere. As if there was no such thing as a state of rest for these people, merely constant motion.

Various vehicles also crowded the street, moving all of two miles an hour. These humans were so proud of their internal combustion engines. He'd like to see a human try travelling the stars by gliding on celestial ether. Then he'd be impressed.

As Cthulhu wandered the streets, he happened upon an ornamental water fountain. It was beautifully ornate, but its beauty was marred by the sight of several humans dressed in tattered clothes laying about its base.

Wondering what these humans could be possibly doing, Cthulhu ventured closer. One of the humans called out to him from the ground.

"Hey, mister," the man said, bearing a slight speech impediment. "Can ya spare some change?"

Cthulhu searched his vocabulary; change... transition? Transformation? This man could certainly do with a change in appearance... but what did he expect Cthulhu to do about that?

Cthulhu cocked his head in confusion.

"Money," said the poorly man. "Ya got money?"

Ah, money. This man wanted Cthulhu to give him

money.

But he didn't have any. In fact, the whole human currency system was completely alien to him. He had to tell the man that he was not from here. Alien, so to speak.

A word for alien, foreign...

"I'm Cthulhu," Cthulhu said. That would be adequate, wouldn't it?

"Cthulhu, huh?" said the poor man. "You African or something?"

No, I'm not African, you ignorant cretin! Cthulhu thought.

"I'm Cthulhu," Cthulhu persisted.

"Whatsamatta wit you? Ya deaf 'r somethin'?"

Cthulhu was beginning to wonder the same thing about the poorly clothed human before him. Instead of continuing his endeavour to try to communicate with the man, Cthulhu simply said, "bye," and turned from the man, moving away from the fountain. Cthulhu briefly saw the man raise his hand, extending one of his bony fingers, jerking it into the air as if stabbing something. Cthulhu had not been taught this gesture, and therefore was ignorant to its meaning. He stored the image away to ask Natty about later.

===

Another building, another sense of terror. But this one was different, in that there were many, many more people swarming about this structure called a "department store." It was disturbingly reminiscent of a nest of social insects, patrons constantly entering an exiting. The cold Autumn wind whipped at Cthulhu as he reluctantly stepped through another one of those accursed revolving doors.

Once inside, Cthulhu found the department store to be vast, spacious, with a brilliant marble floor and lights that hung from the high ceiling. It reminded Cthulhu of a great hall of his people (albeit slightly drier), except for those strange moving staircases...

Cthulhu cautiously stepped toward the moving staircase, placed a single foot upon a step that, before Cthulhu had time to withdraw, carried his foot upward. Stuck in an awkward position, Cthulhu continued his ascent until he was doing a split, riding slowly to the next floor.

When he arrived at the top, sanity and dignity barely intact, Cthulhu found himself once again surrounded by people. One area nearest to him was labelled "Perfumery," which Cthulhu had no comprehension of.

But it certainly smelled good.

He headed towards the Perfumery, and as soon as he entered the department, he was confronted by a small female human. She held in her hand a small bottle.

"Would you care to sample our new passion fruit spray, sir?"

Cthulhu looked at the bottle she held out to him.

Passion fruit? Spray?

Fruit...

Fruit!

Food!

The woman was offering him a sort of food...

Cthulhu took the awkward container in his hand, lifted his mask slightly, sprayed the liquid onto his taste tentacle.

The woman looked shocked.

A tingling, burning sensation filled Cthulhu's head, his brain, spread throughout his body.

The small human cringed slightly as Cthulhu growled in delight.

Before he was even fully aware of what he was doing, Cthulhu quickly undid the top of the bottle, swallowed the entire contents.

When Cthulhu found there was none left in the bottle, he quickly went to one of the shelves, grabbed another bottle, emptied it.

Whatever this substance was, it rivalled even his people's finest wines.

===

By the time store security arrived, he'd emptied the contents of nearly every perfume bottle. They found him in the process of prying the top off of a bottle of White Diamonds and shouted at him to halt.

"I am Cthulhu!!!" The Star-Spawn shouted, raising his fingers in the gesture used by the transient he had met previously.

With that, he passed out.

==

Natty's workday was going very well. She had a position as a teller, and she was probably one of the only polite ones you could find on the island. She had just finished helping a customer with a deposit when her cell phone rang. She checked the caller ID;

TPD 6TH PRCNCT

The police department?

Natty pressed answered the call with a shaky, "Hello?"

"Natty!" said a slurred, raspy voice.

Natty couldn't breathe; The voice could belong to nobody else but...

==

At the 6th Precinct, Cthulhu had such a large

headache that he could hardly maintain his grip on the phone's handset. It was a wonder he had remembered Natty's cell phone number.

"Cthulhu? What're you doing there?"

Cthulhu painfully racked his brain for the right words.

"At cop house. Got... crapulous... from smell-good stuff. Need me get out."

"Got... what?"

Cthulhu became agitated.

"Drunk! I have got drunk!"

"Alright, alright. I'll be down there shortly."

Cthulhu felt relieved, but he still had that hideous headache.

==

Cthulhu lay on Natty's soft, blue-leather couch. It creaked slightly under his weight as he held a large bag of ice to his forehead. Natty sat on the couch next to him.

"You're lucky I have a hefty inheritance, or else I'd've never been able to pay that bail."

Cthulhu grunted in reply, his mind still clouded from his "perfumery massacre."

"So you really drank a whole perfumery?"

Cthulhu nodded.

"So much for keeping a low profile."

DID YOU KNOW?!?!?

Due to the fact that a Cthulhi's taste and smell organs, as well as their corresponding brain centres, are nearly one in the same, it is possible for said Cthulhi to become intoxicated by any substance with a strong enough smell.

When a Cthulhi ingests said powerful-smelling substance, their nerve impulses rapidly alternate between the parallel neurons, causing confusion, nausea, and intense, crippling headaches.

V

In Which Cthulhu Participates in Halloween

==

THRESHOLD ISLAND, OCTOBER 31

Cthulhu wasn't very happy right now.

Here he was, wandering through the street once more, but at least the previous time he had retained a sliver of dignity.

Cthulhu did not enjoy being dressed in a tattered navy overcoat. He did not enjoy the fact that he wore a ridiculously big tricorn hat. And he especially did not enjoy the idea of walking around the city without his mask on.

He strode, smouldering, with Natty at his side. She was dressed as tamely as Cthulhu was extravagant; Natty was clad in a flowing, black, Japanese-styled robe which was embellished with a white belt, to which was secured one of Natty's own katana. From what she had told Cthulhu, she was a character from a television series Cthulhu had never seen.

As another person passed them, Natty said, "Happy Halloween."

"I'm Davy Jones," Cthulhu intoned.

"Cthulhu, how many times do I have to say it," Natty said, becoming a little irritated with her companion. "Everyone can see you're Davy Jones. Say 'Happy Halloween'."

"Why?"

"Because it's Halloween."

A pause.

"Why?"

Natty groaned in annoyance.

"Why I cannot say 'Do you fear death?' That what Davy Jones say."

"That would suit you."

"Then I can says it?"

"No."

==

Wal-Mart: the store that owns everything.

Or so Cthulhu had been told.

It loomed before them almost the same way that department store did, but Wal-Mart was labelled with its own name by enormous bold-faced letters over its entrance.

"Why we here, Natty?"

"Because Halloween means candy prices are way lower."

Cthulhu logged this definition away for future reference. "Halloween" was much easier to say than "candy prices are way lower."

==

Wal-Mart wasn't half as bad as the department store; firstly because there were none of those infernal moving staircases, and then because there wasn't a perfumery anywhere nearby.

On the way to the candy aisle, Cthulhu caught a glimpse of something in the home entertainment department.

On a screen, a man dressed in plated armour, using a cutting tool as an improvised weapon, cutting down hordes of undead beings.

Cthulhu moved towards the screen in a trance-like daze.

"Cthulhu? The candy aisle's this way..."

Cthulhu didn't hear her, so when he reached the aisle containing the screen, he wasn't expecting Natty to come up behind him and give him a sharp smack to the back of the head.

Snapping out of his reverie of wonder, Cthulhu

turned to her, growling sharply.

"What do you think you're doing, Cthulhu?"

Cthulhu pointed to the screen. Below it, a teenage boy of about fourteen held a form of interface control device.

"What that?"

Natty looked at the screen.

"That's *Dead Space*."

"*Dead Space*," Cthulhu repeated reverently.

"Yeah."

"What is it?"

"A video game. You take that controller, and you use it to move the character and dismember the zombies."

Cthulhu stared once more in wonderment at the screen. A few more zombies were mercilessly dismembered.

Cthulhu moved to the kid at the controls, roughly shoved the boy aside.

"Happy Halloween," said Cthulhu.

The boy casually favoured Cthulhu with a now-familiar hand gesture, and sulked out of sight.

It took a while, but Cthulhu got the hang of the strange Xbox controls, and was blowing away Necromorphs in no time. Natty watched in bewilderment as Cthulhu completely destroyed the game, almost like an experienced game player.

After about an hour and a half, Natty finally told

Cthulhu that it was time to go. Cthulhu was torn that he had to leave his newly discovered friend; the Xbox.

===

Natty and Cthulhu left Wal-Mart with the bounty of their Halloween.

Natty with a bag filled to the top with candy.

Cthulhu, however, carried a box with a green "X" marking it.

He was very happy right now.

DID YOU KNOW?!?!?

From a recent survey, the highest-rated and most played games on Threshold island are:

10. *Evil Dead: Fistful of Boomstick*

9. *Soul Calibur: Universe*

8. Dark Corners of the Earth

7. Half-Life 2

6. *Slayer Girl in Broken World*

5. *Infamous Alien*

4. *Blade Runner: the Official Game*

3. *Halo: Combat Evolved*

2. *Halo: Reach*

1. *Dead Space*

VI

In Which Cthulhu Gets a Call

==

THRESHOLD ISLAND, NOVEMBER 22

"I don't like this," said Cthulhu, shifting uncomfortably. He was dressed in his best human clothes; which happened to be blue jeans, a leather belt, and a black "Highlander" T-shirt with lyrics to Queen's "Princes of the Universe" emblazoned across it. His mask was, by necessity, in place, and his wings occupied an otherwise empty backpack slung over his shoulders.

"Cthulhu, it's no different from going out in public. You even know enough English now to be convincing as a normal human."

"Yes, but..."

"But what?"

A pause.

"I don't like it..."

Natty rolled her eyes in annoyance. Cthulhu was a proud warrior, but she couldn't help likening him at times to a very small child. It was quite cute, actually.

"I've gotta check on the yams."

Natty moved into the kitchen. A smell reached Cthulhu that made the Star-Spawn sigh.

"With marshmallows?" asked the Cthulhi.

"Of course," called Natty from the kitchen.

The doorbell rang, and Cthulhu turned, reaching to his back, trying to unsheathe a sword that wasn't there. He was *that* tense.

"That's probably them, Cthulhu. Go ahead and answer the door."

Cthulhu looked speculatively in the direction of the kitchen, but moved toward the door nonetheless.

When Cthulhu opened the door, before him stood two people—one was a female, the other a male. They both looked to be about Natty's age. The male's gaze was previously somewhere in the vicinity of Cthulhu's abdomen, as he was expecting someone a bit shorter. His eyes drifted up to Cthulhu's face, finding the almost death's-head of a face more than a bit disconcerting. The surgical mask didn't help the impression, much.

"H-hi," said the man nervously. "I'm Joel."

"Joel White?" asked Cthulhu.

"Yeah..." the man smiled. "You must be Cthulhu."

"Yes I am."

"Natty's told me a lot about you," said Joel, extending a hand, "I'm Asenath's brother."

"Yes, I know." Cthulhu took the man's hand, shook it. Joel winced a bit at the Cthulhi's strong grip.

"This is my girlfriend, Rachael."

The female human now extended her hand. Cthulhu shook it a bit more gently than he had Joel's.

"A pleasure," Cthulhu said.

"The same," replied Rachael.

At that time, Natty came up from behind Cthulhu.

"Joel!" she said, embracing her brother in a warm hug.

"Good to see you, Natty."

"I see you've already met Cthulhu."

"Yeah," Joel said, flexing his slightly sore hand a bit. "We've met."

"Rachael!" Natty cried, turning and embracing the other woman. "It's been too long."

Rachael returned her hug warmly, saying, "I'm so glad we could make it. Thanks for inviting us."

"It's just too bad Mum and Kelly can't be here," Natty said.

"Kelly? Leave Florida? Not likely. She might lose her tan," Joel said sardonically.

"Well, maybe everybody can get together for

Christmas," Rachael said. "Maybe we could all go visit them and get tan for Christmas."

"That would be great," Natty said, wondering how that would ever work out.

"So," Joel asked impatiently. "Are we gonna eat, or what?"

===

The turkey was huge. It was the biggest turkey Natty could buy. And it looked as tender as a bird could get.

But that wasn't what Cthulhu was eyeing.

It was those candied yams.

"*Yams,*" sung a heavenly voice from above. But Cthulhu was pretty sure it was his imagination.

They looked divine, the colour of a golden sunset, as Natty set them almost exactly in front of Cthulhu. Before Cthulhu could stop himself, his hand involuntarily moved toward the tray. Just before his fingers touched the marshmallows, a hand smacked his away. Natty was the owner of this hand.

"Not yet."

Cthulhu uttered some Elder-Tongue curses under his breath as he rubbed his hand.

"Would you carve the turkey, Cthulhu?"

Here's one thing Cthulhu was good with; blades. He deftly picked up the large carving knife, began to sharpen its blade. With smooth, fluid motions, he carved slices from the turkey, using knife and fork to serve some to each of the people at the table. Natty spooned a small heap of stuffing onto everyone's plate.

As calmly as he could, Cthulhu dug into his plate.

"So, Cthulhu," Joel said after a short silence. "What exactly do you do?"

"Do?" Cthulhu cast a glance at Natty, who nodded. "I do video games."

Joel looked slightly confused.

"He makes video games," clarified Natty.

"Yes. Make video games."

"Which ones have you made?"

"Um," said Cthulhu. "None yet."

"Haven't sold any ideas. He's on the market," said Natty.

"Hmm. I see," said Joel, turning back to his turkey.

After another short silence, the phone rang. Natty began to stand, but Cthulhu made a gesture to stop her.

"No. I get it."

Cthulhu stood from the table, walked over to the phone. He picked it up; put it to the side of his head.

"Hello?"

"Hello E'nasa," said a calm, centred voice from the other end.

Cthulhu nearly dropped the phone.

"You know me?"

"Just what you are. And what you aren't; human. Tell me, do you miss R'lyeh?"

Cthulhu made no reply.

"Sorry, I forgot you've probably never seen it. Mi-Go invasion's a pretty nasty thing, isn't it?"

"Who are you?"

"That's not important. Walk to your TV."

Cthulhu did so. It was a replay of the Macy's parade in New York.

"Switch it to channel fifteen; CNN."

Cthulhu picked up the remote, clicked it a few times.

"The cause of death is still not apparent to the police, but it is speculated that murder with some sort of heavy weapon is involved..."

The screen depicted a murder scene, yellow tape spread everywhere, people crowding around. In the centre lay a man, about thirty years of age. His mouth was open in a rictus of agony.

His entire torso had been completely... excised. His limbs looked limp and rubbery. All told, it seemed as if something had been wearing the man, and had removed him like a jumpsuit.

"It could be a false alarm, but if I were you, I wouldn't take the chance."

Cthulhu could almost see the man on the other end smirking. In fact, he could see him smirking; on the TV screen, a man in the crowd was speaking on a cell phone. He was dressed in a long, brown trenchcoat, matted dark-brown hair, a nose a bit too big for his face. He was smiling.

His mouth moved in unison to the words on the phone. He looked right at the camera.

"I'll be watching you."

Cthulhu suddenly owed Natty a new phone; this one had been reduced to a fistful of plastic shards.

DID YOU KNOW?!?!?

Mi-Go biology is not, at this time, fully understood. What is known is that they do not have a single given form, and do not conform to any biological phylum.

Mi-Go reproduction takes place when a sample of Mi-Go biological material enters the body of a sentient organism. The tissue will develop its own nervous system, using the host's genetic material for sustenance.

When at a suitable stage of development, the Mi-Go larva will emerge, fully formed, from the host's body. The host's internal organs will be totally consumed, leaving the host a lifeless shell.

VII

In Which Cthulhu is Introduced to the Concept of the Holiday Rush

==

THRESHOLD ISLAND, DECEMBER 18

"**H**appy Christ-Mass," said Cthulhu—as well as he could through the fifteen boxes he was carrying. Natty was really taking her Christmas shopping seriously, as she had a mother, a brother, and a sister (not to mention a space-faring alien charge) to shop for.

As for Cthulhu, he was once again doing his best to blend in, wearing his common attire but also an over-large, bright red Santa hat. Though his main focus was anchored in this store, Cthulhu's thoughts trailed off elsewhere.

That man in the brown coat—how did he know so

much about him? How had he known about the "murder" so quickly? How had he known exactly what channel would be broadcasting the report? And were the Mi-Go actually in Threshold? How had they gotten there? Too many questions that Cthulhu didn't have the foggiest about solving. He knew he should tell Natty, but it seemed she was lost in the festivities. Perhaps he could find a solution by his lonesome.

As Natty and Cthulhu browsed the isle, Natty paused, looking at some DVDs that were for sale.

"How much more, Natty?"

"Not too much more. I just found out that my entire family's coming here for Christmas, and I haven't gotten any of my shopping done, yet."

Cthulhu could never grasp the distinctly human concept of procrastination.

Natty held up two DVDs for Cthulhu's consideration.

"Do you think Joel would like "Monty Python's Flying Circus" or "Evil Dead II" better?"

As Cthulhu was a Monty Python fan himself and wasn't too keen on that Bruce Campbell person, he pointed at the first option. Natty threw the DVD on top of the rapidly forming pile, adding a few more ounces to Cthulhu's load.

"I think this enough, Natty."

"Yeah, I know. We're heading for the checkout

now."

Cthulhu definitely needed to be told his current position; it was a wonder Natty wasn't leading him by the hand, right now.

"I need to do my shopping for you, too, you know," said Natty.

"Yes, I know."

But what could she possibly get him? A blade? A gun? A ticket off this dirt-clod? In actuality, he didn't want her to get him anything; she already provided his food and shelter, and what was becoming increasingly more important on this hostile world; friendship.

So what could he get her? Perhaps a bottle of perfume would be nice...

==

Walking along the snow/slush-covered side-walk, Cthulhu's load had lessened slightly, as Natty was now carrying a few of the packages. Cthulhu was thankful for the slight reprieve.

"Thanks for helping out, Cthulhu."

Cthulhu growled in response. Natty continued;

"I'll try and get a cab; you wait here."

As she went to flag down a taxi, something caught Cthulhu's eye. It was a TV in the window of a Radio Shack, displaying the local news.

"Police are still searching for the alleged killer involved with two seemingly connected deaths in the past few weeks."

She had to know.

"Natty," called Cthulhu. "Come see this."

As she came up to him, she asked, "What is it, Cthulhu?"

Her attention was then drawn to the report.

"Both murder victims were violently killed seemingly by having their organs violently torn out."

Natty, her jaw on the floor, looked at Cthulhu, who nodded.

"It was suspected earlier that the wound was caused by a large firearm, but such suspicions were dispelled by the coroner, who stated that firstly, the wound protruded outward, as if from within, and secondly, the cadaver's internal organs seemed to have been liquefied."

"On another note, the recent disappearances attributed to the coastal town of Innsmouth, Massachusetts..."

Cthulhu didn't catch the rest of the report.

"Cthulhu, you don't think..."

Cthulhu didn't answer. He simply turned from her, caught a taxi by roaring loudly at it. Natty and Cthulhu got in the cab, the driver looking rather nervous, casting uneasy glances at Cthulhu's mask as Natty gave the man instructions on their destination.

As they were driving, the radio drew Cthulhu's attention.

"This next song goes out to Cthulhu, from 'a friend'," the announcer said.

Cthulhu leaned forward in his seat, his eyes wide.

"*We can be heroes*," said the radio. "*Just for one day...*"

DID YOU KNOW?!?!?

ETBS, the particular radio station that Cthulhu was listening to in the taxi, does not take requests.

VIII

In Which Cthulhu is Further Vexed by Awkward Moments, and There is Also Much Christmas

==

THRESHOLD ISLAND, DECEMBER 24

The room was dark, dimmed to the taste of the Cthulhi who occupied it. Cthulhu currently sat at the elaborate desk he had purchased a month ago. It was solid polished marble, as Cthulhu specifically chose because it reminded him of home. He used a pair of over-large scissors to cut yet another clipping from a newspaper. He pinned it up on his bulletin board next to the others—

"BIZZARE CHAIN OF MURDERS"

"GRISLY 'DISEMBOWLER' SERIAL KILLER STRIKES AGAIN"

"12 FOUND DEAD IN 8TH STREET ALLEY"

"SEWER WORKERS DISSAPEAR—LINK TO SERIAL KILLINGS SUSPECTED"

and the newest; "SEWER WORKERS STILL MISSING—SEARCH PARTIES YIELD NO RESULTS"

Cthulhu had been monitoring the reports for days now. He was now eighty-five percent sure that the Mi-Go were now in Threshold.

What he was going to do about it was the real problem.

Cthulhu was a warrior, but he was hardly a match for what seemed to be a considerable number of Mi-Go.

As he was pondering this, the door to his room opened, a beam of light cutting the darkness.

"Cthulhu," said Natty from the doorway. "Our guests should be here any time now. You might wanna get dressed."

At the time, Cthulhu was only dressed in his native attire; a tight loincloth his people called a "bl'ei." Natty did not seem the least bit embarrassed at seeing Cthulhu's exposed body. In fact, she seemed slyly amused.

"Get out," he said simply.

"Why?"

"I'm... naked."

"You're only partially naked."

"It still count."

"Okay, fine. But hurry up, they should be here any minute."

===

The doorbell rang, and this time Natty was available to answer it. When she opened the door, Cthulhu saw two women holding gift-wrapped boxes. One was much older – perhaps late-forties – than Natty, with pale skin and grey streaks in her black hair. The other was slightly younger than Natty, with dark brown hair and much tanner skin than Natty herself. She was dressed in a very thick winter coat, and looked like she had been freezing to death.

"Kelly! Mum!"

Natty hugged her mother, then her sister. Cthulhu noticed that the hugs lasted a few seconds longer than the typical, observable human "friendly greeting hug." Cthulhu understood why; Natty didn't see her mother or sister often, for obvious reasons. Her only family would be visiting tonight, including Joel. Her father had died, giving his life in the secret profession he had passed to Natty.

"Good to see you, Natty," said Kelly.

"You too, Kelly. How's Threshold treating you?"

"Treating me? It won't leave me alone. I think I'm gonna catch my death out here."

"Kelly," said Natty's mother. "It's thirty degrees out."

"Yeah," replied Kelly. "It's below freezing! It's miserable."

Natty rolled her eyes; Kelly didn't have that tan for no reason. She normally lived in Florida. She didn't have much of the adventuresome/murderesome spirit that Natty had in common with Cthulhu, and that she'd inherited from her father.

"So," said Natty's mother. "Where's that friend of yours you've been talking about so much?"

"Yeah, he sounds hot," Kelly said.

Natty blushed a little. Mostly from Kelly's blatancy, but also in regards to the fact that she shared her sister's opinion.

"Yeah," said Natty, snapping out of it. "He's just inside. In fact, he's—"

"Right here."

Cthulhu, a master of stealth – despite being seven feet tall, dressed in extra large jeans and a huge, long-sleeved, black dress shirt that was extremely tight around his back – had seemed invisible until this moment. His death-stare looked a little softer because of the huge Santa hat he now had on. He seemed to like wearing it.

"Pleasure to meet you, Mrs. and Ms. White."

Natty's mother looked rather shocked, but Kelly's eyes were wide, and she slowly walked forward in a trance-like daze.

"Charmed, I'm sure..." she said in an equally trance-like voice.

She moved up next to Cthulhu, batting her eyelashes.

"I'm Kelly," she said, a little too pleasantly for Natty's tastes.

"I know," Cthulhu replied bluntly.

"Wanna know more?"

"Okay," Natty said suddenly, taking Kelly by the shoulders and moving her away from Cthulhu. "There'll be no knowing here."

Cthulhu simply walked over to the couch, sat down, and turned on the TV. He flipped through the channels every five seconds, obviously looking for something in particular.

"Where did you say you met him?" asked Natty's mother.

"Um... on a visit to Arkham. I was doing a bit of freelance work."

And every bit of it was truth. Of course, she neglected to mention the fact that he was a space-faring soldier, or that she was in Arkham to slaughter aliens and monsters. But Natty didn't really believe that this kind of omission was the same as lying.

"Where's he from?" asked Kelly, noting the odd coloration of his skin (which she found bizarrely attractive).

"Rhode Island," said Cthulhu without turning from the television.

"Ah," said Kelly. "That's interesting."

"So," Natty said, pointedly digressing. "When are Joel and Rachael gonna be here?"

Natty's mum said, "Joel just called. They'll be here any minute."

"While we're waiting, would anyone like some eggnog?"

Cthulhu immediately raised his hand.

"I know you do, Cthulhu. I meant Mum and Kelly."

Cthulhu dropped his hand, his shoulders slumping.

"I wouldn't mind some," said Mum.

"Me, too," said Kelly.

Natty moved over to a table where she had set a bottle of eggnog and six champagne glasses. She filled three of the glasses, handed one to Kelly, one to her mother, and one to Cthulhu, who took it a little more eagerly than he should have. It was at that time that the doorbell rang.

"I'll get it," said Natty. "It must be Joel and Rachael."

She walked over, opened the door. Before her stood not her brother and his girlfriend, but a man dressed in a dark brown leather trench-coat, tan pants and a red dress shirt. His brown hair was matted beyond recognition and fell in knots in front of his deeply shadowed eyes. He looked like he hadn't slept for weeks.

"Hey," the rather young man said, his juvenile voice carrying a heavy smell of coffee. "I'm a friend of Cthulhu's."

"I don't know you," said Natty.

"But I know you, Asenath Thurston White."

Natty was more than a bit freaked out.

"What do you want?"

"To come in," said the Coated Man pleasantly. He held up a large, gift wrapped box that smelled faintly of strong coffee. Natty had somehow failed to notice it before. "I got Cthulhu a present," the Coated Man grinned.

"Alright," said Natty reluctantly. "Come on in."

She gestured past her, and the Coated Man stepped rather gracefully and regally inside.

"Sorry I couldn't get you one," he said, placing the box under the large Christmas tree. "I've sort of fallen on hard times, you see..."

He walked up to where Cthulhu was sitting, placed a hand on his shoulder. Cthulhu looked up, saw the Coated Man's face. His blood froze in his veins.

"Hello," he managed.

"Natty; are you going to introduce your friend?" Mum asked. Kelly was looking at the newcomer with an expression that was a disturbing combination of predatory and entranced.

"Of course," Natty said. "Mum, Kelly, this is

Cthulhu's friend... um..."

"Lovecraft is my name," the Coated Man replied courteously. "Art design is my game, if you'll pardon the pun. I work for a small, independent video game developer and I'm currently trying to get Cthulhu here a job." Then, directed at Cthulhu, "Sitting around playing *Dead Space* and watching CNN doesn't pay much, good buddy."

Cthulhu glared at Lovecraft, but managed to sound pleasant.

"Yes," he said. "Doesn't pay at all."

==

Frank Sinatra was singing "Silent Night" on a CD that was playing when the doorbell rang again.

"I'll get it," said Natty, silently hoping for no more surprises.

She opened the door, revealing Joel and Rachael, carrying some more presents.

"Joel, Rachael. Great to see you!"

"You too, Natty. Where can we put these?" said Joel.

"Oh, right under the tree in here," said Natty, taking some of the boxes. They moved to put them under the tree, briefly passing the couch where Kelly and Lovecraft sat, the former slowly sliding toward the latter. Lovecraft indifferently watched the television, which was currently playing the Saturday Night Live Christmas Special. Cthulhu had moved away from Lovecraft, to the table next to the Christmas tree, where he nicked another cookie from the tray. The CD switched to Bing Crosby singing "White Christmas."

"So," said Joel, ever in a hurry. "When're we gonna open these?"

"Patience Joel," replied Natty. "Patience."

She went to get another bottle of eggnog, as Cthulhu had finished off the original one. As she was headed for the kitchen, she bumped right into Cthulhu. Before either of them could move, Joel said, "Yo, Natty! You and Cthulhu are under the mistletoe!"

Natty and Cthulhu both looked up, seeing the bright red and green plant hanging over their heads. Natty didn't remember putting up any mistletoe, and neither did Cthulhu.

On the couch, Lovecraft smirked.

"Aren't you gonna kiss him?" remarked Rachael.

Natty nodded briefly, looked at Cthulhu, who's jet-black eyes were widening to the size of softballs.

Natty leaned forward, kissed Cthulhu on the mask.

"Come on," said Joel. "That's not a kiss."

"I haven't heard you cough once since I met you," Rachael said. "So you can't really be sick. Take off the mask."

A brief mental image flashed through both Cthulhu and Natty's minds of a kiss shared between them without the moderation of a surgical mask.

"NO," cried the two in unison.

"Um, part of his... religion," blushed Natty.

"Happy Hanukkah," said Cthulhu quickly.

Confused expressions arose all about the room.

Lovecraft snickered quietly.

"So," Natty said rather suddenly, her face and ears flushed so red she almost appeared to be bleeding. "How about those presents?"

"Yes, presents," said Cthulhu.

After a short time, they took to the gifts. Joel was excited about his Monty Python DVD, but Natty wasn't quite so enthusiastic when she got three pairs of tube socks from her brother in response. He revealed, however, that this was a gag gift. Her real present was a subscription to *Advanced Combat Firearms Weekly*. Natty was exceedingly grateful.

While everyone else was opening their presents, Kelly leaned close to Lovecraft, whispered in his ear.

"I've got a present for you," she said.

"Really?" Lovecraft replied, his gaze never wavering from the TV screen.

He did notice, however, that a small sprig of mistletoe had been raised above his head. He indifferently stared at the TV.

"Merry Christmas," said Kelly.

"That's very nice of you," intoned Lovecraft.

Kelly was somewhat disappointed by his lack of reaction.

"You don't talk much, do you?"

This time, Lovecraft looked directly at her, his dark eyes seeming even darker within his expressionless face.

"No," he said simply.

"Oh, if you wanna be *that* way," replied Kelly, disappointed.

Back at the tree, Cthulhu had just finished opening his present from Natty (a very large bottle of perfume), when he came to a huge box, wrapped in Transformers print paper (the original series, not that Michael Bay monstrosity).

The tag read "To: Cthulhu, From: the guy who's getting hit on by Natty's sister."

Cthulhu looked to the couch, saw Kelly particularly close to Lovecraft. The boy nodded to Cthulhu, smirked. Cthulhu looked back at the tag, read it again.

How did he...?

Lovecraft nodded at him once more, and Cthulhu began to tear away the garish wrapping paper. When he finished, he slowly lifted the lid, half-expecting a Byakhee bat to leap out and gnaw on his face.

He didn't get a Byakhee, but something equally surprising.

Inside the rather large box was a whole Cthulhi *arsenal*.

Triple-barrelled scattergun, motorized spinblade, thirty-nine and a half feet of razor-cord, and even a segmented longblade...

Cthulhu quickly closed the box, stood up.

"Cthulhu, what's—"

Before Natty could say anything else, he had run to the couch, gift box under one arm, grabbed Lovecraft by the arm, and rushed out of the room.

"What was that all about?" asked a very confused Joel.

===

Cthulhu slammed the door to his room, threw Lovecraft to the floor. He grabbed the scattergun from the box (which should not have been physically possible, because the scattergun was three feet long, and the box was only two) and waved it in Lovecraft's face.

"Where—Where you get this!?!" he roared.

The Lovecraft simply stared coolly at him, his expressionless gaze only wavered by that accursed smirk.

"A friend I like to call Gray, but you probably know him as R'lsek. He's spec-ops, isn't he? Long-range clean-up. Set to be promoted to an Elder soon, right?"

Cthulhu was shocked. He knew R'lsek, and had even trained under him once. He was a fierce soldier and a bit of a legend.

Cthulhu grabbed Lovecraft by his shirt, hoisted him to his feet.

"How you know R'lsek?"

"Well, that's for me to know and well..." he smirked. "Well, you *not* to."

"Who are you?"

"No one of consequence."

"I need to know!"

"Get used to disappointment."

Lovecraft ran to the window (which was now open, for some reason), placed one foot on the sill in a regal pose. He produced a small sheet of paper.

"If you ever need my assistance, this is my cell number. I'm always available."

Cthulhu looked at the paper; it read "8201890."

"My friend," said Lovecraft, "this is the day you shall always remember as the day you almost caught —"

With that, the man rather unceremoniously tripped and fell backwards out the window. Cthulhu dashed to the window, leaned almost halfway out.

There was absolutely no sign of Lovecraft; just the busy Threshold traffic below. Cthulhu leaned back in the window, growling. He crumpled the piece of paper and shoved it into his pocket.

==

Cthulhu exited his room to find that things were much tamer in the living room. The light was dim, lit by glowing candlelight. The TV played a news bit about Santa's safe take-off this year. Joel and Rachael were snuggled together on the couch, Natty sitting a short distance from them. Cthulhu looked at the clock on the wall: "12:01". It was Christmas.

Cthulhu moved to the couch, sat next to Natty.

A very interesting first Christmas for the Cthulhi. Very interesting indeed.

DID YOU KNOW?!?!?

Natty's father, Thurston White, was the C.E.O. of White House Publishing, Inc. While legitimate and profitable, this was, for the most part, a front business for White's true profession: the systematic hunting and slaughtering of eldrich creatures. A profession that he kept hidden from all but his eldest daughter, who also held the role of his apprentice.

IX

In Which More Protagonists Are Introduced, as well as a New Antagonist.

==

INNSMOUTH, MASSACHUSETTS, AN INDETERMINATE POINT IN TIME

Zoë Allen couldn't sleep. Four hours ago, she had checked into the Gilman House Inn, and she had been given the key to a rather musty room on the top floor that didn't even have a bathroom. She had lain on the spongy bed for some time, trying to read the book she had brought with her. But the book could not distract her from the feeling of unease she'd felt since she'd first arrived in Innsmouth.

Zoë was seventeen years of age, with straight, light-brown hair. She was considered pretty, but she considered herself quite average.

She hadn't even intended to stop at this rotted, creepy town on her way to Arkham. She was supposed to be meeting with Jenny and Marsha for Frank Wayland's going away party the day after tomorrow. But instead, she decided at the last minute that it would be a good idea to visit her great uncle Zadok on the way.

So she had got off the bus at Innsmouth, where people stared at you with bulgy eyes and everywhere you went reeked of fish. On top of that, after what seemed like an eternity of searching, she couldn't find Uncle Zadok anywhere. Finally, she'd given up the search and decided to stay the night at what had seemed like a fairly decent little inn.

But that was hours ago. Before she started hearing the noises.

Zoë was an unusually self-reliant young woman, but now she sat on her bed, her knees hugged to her chest. Outside her room, down at the street level, she could hear things she didn't want to; screams, crashing, horrible animal sounds that she couldn't place.

She had turned off her light, because in addition to the sounds in the street, she could now hear footsteps. Footsteps approaching her door.

She could see it, now; the door knob, jiggling, testing. She had locked it, but whoever it was probably had a key.

Keys rattled, and the knob turned. Zoë had jammed it with a chair, driving whoever was trying to get in to agitation. They began to pound on the door.

Zoë was at the window. She opened it. The streets below held no type of hellish fury; those sounds came from elsewhere in the town. There was a ledge, but just barely. She could inch along it, climb the drainpipe graciously provided for her.

The night air biting at her skin (she was in her nightclothes), she made her way out onto the ledge. The building was only two stories – a dangerous fall, but not lethal.

Probably break a leg, though, Zoë thought.

The drainpipe wasn't too cold, and Zoë jumped to it from the ledge, just barely managing to hold on. She began to curse herself with several obscene words for her stupidity.

"I'm not doing this," she told herself. "I am *so* not doing this…"

But she was.

As she ponderously slid down the pipe, she suddenly heard a violent crash within her room; they'd broken down the door.

Should've closed the freaking window, Zoë thought, cursing herself again.

Zoë was halfway down the side of the building when she suddenly saw a dark figure appear above her. In its hand was a gleaming silver object.

She heard a sharp sound that she identified as suppressed gunfire, and felt whatever had been fired streak past her head.

Startled, she lost her grip on the pipe and landed painfully on her back, her head thankfully not impacting with the side walk.

Fuelled by adrenaline from the bullets being fired, Zoë picked herself up and sprinted away.

Why're they shooting at me? Zoë thought.

The way the locals looked at her, however, she figured they must have some weird vendetta against outsiders. Possibly a murderous vendetta.

She suddenly got an awful suspicion regarding what happened to Uncle Zadok.

That meant she couldn't trust anyone. She'd have to find a way to get out of town. Maybe find a car that had its keys in it, or hot-wire it...

What was she thinking? She wasn't a delinquent. She had no idea where to even start in hijacking a vehicle. But, it was her only option, and she had to try.

Making her way through alleys, shadowed from the strangely harsh moonlight, she finally found a parking lot for a dilapidated theatre. A single Chevy pickup was parked right next to the entrance.

Running to it, she picked up a discarded boot and smashed in the window. She quickly dropped the boot when she realized that is was covered in thick mucous and smelled of fish. She was about to wipe her hands off when a stream of the same viscous material dripped onto her shoulder. She looked up slowly toward the source.

On top of the canopy of the theatre's entrance was a figure, silhouetted by the moonlight. Bipedal, but decidedly inhuman. She could just make out what looked like fins on either side of its head, and those yellow, luminescent eyes...

The beast leapt at her, landed on her, her head smashing against the asphalt.

And Zoë Allen blacked out.

===

The town was overrun, and R'lsek knew it. He stood atop the building that previously served as the town's place of worship (since converted to a meeting place for cultists), surveying the situation. The Deep Ones had always been known to favour Innsmouth, and until recently had only taken one or two of the human population per year. But something had them incensed, wild, uncontrollable. Something was affecting their normally calculating minds, rendering them simple, mindless beasts.

Regardless as to whether it was their fault, they would have to be dealt with. At the rate they were spreading, they would cover the entire continent in a few months. The only option left was a total thermal cleansing. It would cost the human population of Innsmouth, but then again, many of them weren't entirely human.

R'lsek felt regretful of the collateral damage, but felt justified in his belief that some must be sacrificed to spare the rest.

R'lsek heard a low growl behind him, slowly tilted his head.

Behind him was a Deep One, a male, about eight feet full height. Its rows of teeth extended gruesomely as its luminous eyes twitched on their stalks. The Deep One, in summary, looked to be a hybrid of a man, a shark, and a deep-sea angler fish.

As the Deep One lunged forward, R'lsek spun, drew the broadsword from his coat, swung it in a tight arc. As it made contact with the creature's neck, the motorized chain blade activated, messily severing the Deep One's head. The head fell with a wet thud, but the body merely slumped. R'lsek looked down, saw the Deep One's razor-claw sticking into his chest.

Then R'lsek blacked out.

DID YOU KNOW?!?!?

Innsmouth, Massachusetts has long been on the verge of implosion. The only thing that keeps it from total destruction is the surprisingly abundant fishing economy, which began back in the early 1800s with the town's settling. It is commonly rumoured that town founder Obed Marsh created a pact with the Deep Ones that if he allowed them to mate with the townspeople, then the business would continue to prosper.

Evidently, this is entirely true.

X

In Which Secrets Are Revealed.

==

THRESHOLD ISLAND, JANUARY 3

R'lsek dropped to the floor, the rain pounding his pale-grey face. He felt nothing as the rain ran into his dead, white eye over which crossed a ragged scar. But his chest burned with white fire as he ponderously picked himself up. He tried to gather his memories into a coherent explanation of the events that had happened. What he got was scattered images of the attack on Innsmouth.

R'lsek checked himself over. Milky white blood dripped profusely from his chest, but otherwise, he was in one piece. His spine was intact, his ribcage, lungs, heart—

Only a flesh wound...

As R'lsek was about to pull out his medical kit to seal the wound, he heard something—he may have been scarred and relatively old, but his senses were still keen enough to detect a single footstep amidst the falling rain.

And a footstep it was, for he turned to see, standing on the edge of the roof, a human boy of about seventeen years, wearing a long, brown coat. The coated boy smirked at R'lsek from a dark-eyed face, reached behind his back, withdrew something, activated it.

It was R'lsek's sword.

The coated boy spun the buzzing blade with machine-like precision, deactivated it, sheathed it in a scabbard at his back.

R'lsek checked his weapon harness. All of his weapons—his sword, scattergun, spinblade, razor cord, even his vial of cauterizing fluid—were gone. He did recall losing most of the items during the skirmish, but many of them had stayed with him until he blacked out.

Before R'lsek had time to react, the coated boy stepped backward off the ledge.

The Cthulhi dashed to the ledge to see a busy street below –

Wait...

A busy street?

He was indeed upon a rooftop, and it was raining,

but he was decidedly not in Innsmouth. R'lsek quickly activated his portable computer, pulled up a map of Earth. His current position was easily several hundred miles from Innsmouth. How could this be? It had been only a matter of minutes ago that he was battling the wretched fishmen.

As he pondered, something caught the corner of his good eye—crouched on a nearby rooftop was a huge, muscular form in full battle-armour. A Cthulhi like himself. He wore a surgical mask, and carried a triple-barrelled scattergun.

R'lsek's very own scattergun.

===

Zoë awoke, dizzy and disoriented. The rain soaked through her pastel-blue nightgown, chilling her skin. It was extremely cold, and she started to shiver. The last thing she remembered was getting attacked by that huge monster—it grabbed her and then... nothing.

She felt as though several hours of her life were missing, as if someone had simply cut them out, or she'd spent the time in an inky blackness.

Her skull throbbed with dull pain, and she reached to feel the back of her head; her fingers returned coloured small traces of red. Half-remembered sensations were stirred up from her subconscious;

foul, somewhat violating memories. She shook them from her mind, heaved herself to her feet. Her joints ached. She was on a side-walk, surrounded by very tall buildings. She had to get inside, or she'd freeze to death...

As she wandered, she noticed that her environs looked nothing like any part of Innsmouth that she had seen during the day. She was studying her surroundings so intently as she walked that she ran straight into a solid object. As both she and the object toppled, Zoë noted that it was not an object, but a teenage boy. He was only around her height, wearing a brown trenchcoat. He in no way resembled the ugly, bulgy-eyed inhabitants of Innsmouth, and thankfully neither did he liken to its fishlike invaders.

"Ummm..." the boy said, his voice coloured with an odd kind of shock as he picked himself up. "Hi."

"Hi," Zoë said, embarrassed to be in her nightclothes and uncertain as to where she even was, and on top of that sprawled on her back on the hold asphalt.

"Here, let me help you up."

He offered a hand, and she accepted it eagerly. He gingerly helped her to her feet. "Are you hurt?"

"No," Zoë blatantly lied.

Zoë took in the boy's appearance: dark eyes and matted hair, wearing a trench-coat standing in the middle of the street. Zoë couldn't hardly think of a more suspicious sight.

"I know I probably look creepy tight now, but you have to believe I only want to help. I know some friends in that building there," he pointed to a large apartment building that was only about ten meters away. "Floor 4, apartment 428. I'll show you."

Zoë was still, of course, apprehensive; this guy was probably either a psychopath or a delinquent. But then, what other choice did she have? Despite the fact that the air did not contain the same biting chill as dank, dreary Innsmouth, it was still too chilly for the way she was dressed. She had to get inside, and this guy didn't really seem the creepy type he looked.

"Alright," she said.

"Follow me," said Lovecraft.

===

R'lsek had no trouble jumping across to the other rooftop undetected by the Cthulhi, and he was now sneaking up next to the other Star-Spawn, unsheathing his combat knife (a half-meter-long blade which his people called a "n'ife"). From a reasonable distance, R'lsek hunkered down, observing the Cthulhi. He seemed to be tracking something; he placed his hand on the ground, brought it up to his face—it was covered with a black, viscous material.

Mi-Go secretion.

Apparently the place he had been transported to had a pest problem as well. What was going on with these creatures?

If the strange, behaviour-altering force was this widespread, he would need the assistance of more troops. Troops which he had absolutely no way of contacting. For now, R'lsek focused on apprehending this single rogue. R'lsek started toward the younger, less wise Cthulhi. The other noticed R'lsek too late, spun around, brandishing R'lsek's scattergun. The soldier knocked the weapon from the rogue's hand, grabbed the younger Cthulhi by the throat. It was then that he clearly saw the youngster's face.

"E'nasa?" he said, dropping the Cthulhi.

"R'lsek!" replied the Star-Spawn known to humans as Cthulhu. He felt as if a burden had been lifted when he began speaking in his native tongue.

R'lsek embraced Cthulhu in a rough yet warm hug (a universal gesture). He abruptly broke the embrace.

"E'nasa, you're..." R'lsek paused, "what're you doing here?

"What do you mean?"

"E'nasa... all troops have been pulled from Earth. The only forces left active are black ops."

"But Elder Dagot —"

"You spoke with Dagot?"

"Yes. Just three months ago."

"Our forces were pulled out in October. That means Dagot stranded you here with no escape, no means of communication. Why would he do that?"

Cthulhu thought back to the last time he'd spoke with Dagot. Something he'd said particularly stood out:

"On the contrary, E'nasa, Asenath here seems just your type."

Dagot, you sly, salty old man.. You were trying to set me up with this human girl, weren't you?

"I have a pretty good idea."

"And?"

"It's rather... embarrassing."

"You're right. You wouldn't want me joking at your expense the rest of our time together."

"Come, I'll show you my home."

===

Meanwhile, back at Natty and Cthulhu's apartment, Natty was minding her own business, watching a rerun of "Mystery Science Theatre 3000." She wasn't really paying attention as Mike and the Bots bashed "Night of the Blood Beast" for the umpteenth time; her thoughts were with Cthulhu.

He was out on a self-assigned mission, attempting to track the Mi-Go for the first time in months. Natty had wanted to go with, but Cthulhu wouldn't let her; there was no telling what would happen if he actually did find a nest. Natty was interrupted in her thoughts by a knock on the door. She had some terrible foreboding that she knew exactly who the knock belonged to. She walked over, opened the door.

Before her stood Lovecraft.

"Hey, Natty. What's up?"

"Why am I not surprised," said Natty, exasperated. At this time, she noticed Zoë standing behind Lovecraft. "Friend of yours?"

"Not really. Her name's Zoë."

Zoë turned quickly, staring in shock at Lovecraft.

"Nice to meet you, I'm Natty," said Natty, extending a hand.

"Zoë," she said, shaking Natty's hand.

"Well, come on in. You must be freezing. I've got some extra clothes in my room you can borrow."

"Thanks."

She allowed Zoë to step past her into the house. Turning back to Natty, she added, "Do you have any aspirin?"

"Sure, the bathroom is just across from the bedroom. The aspirin's in the cabinet."

"Thanks again."

Lovecraft started inside as well, but she stopped him.

"What makes you think you're coming in?"

"Because, well..." he cleared his throat. "May I please come in, Natty?"

Natty looked at him, her expression still rather exasperated.

"Fine, you can come in."

"Thank you," said Lovecraft, walking past her into the apartment.

Natty walked in also, closed the door, "You'll probably end up in here somehow, anyway."

"You're probably right," Lovecraft replied, plopping himself on the couch, saw the MST3K episode on TV. "Hey, I love this one. The original movie had so much potential in its concept, but this stuff's classic."

"Uh-huh," said Natty. "I'm assuming you didn't come here just to watch MST3K."

"How do you know?" Lovecraft said sarcastically.

Natty rolled her eyes.

"But seriously, I came to check on Cthulhu. How's the bug hunt going?"

"Doesn't really surprise me that you know he's out."

Lovecraft grinned widely, "You're finally getting to know me."

"A little better than I'm comfortable with."

"Trust me, you don't know nearly enough."

Zoë entered in from Natty's room, now dressed in a baggy t-shirt and sweat pants. She looked considerably more comfortable, but the ice-bag held to her head betrayed her lingering headache.

"Alright," she said. "Someone's gotta tell me what's goin' on here. Half an hour ago I was in Innsmouth getting attacked by some sort of fish monster and next thing I know I'm laying in the rain in Threshold. Anyone care to elaborate?"

Lovecraft was about to speak, but then paused looked at his watch. Counted down, "three, two, one..."

With "one," the window opened, R'lsek and Cthulhu entering.

"Right on time," said Lovecraft.

R'lsek glared at Lovecraft.

"You again," said Cthulhu. "You ever go away?"

"You!"

Gray had noticed Lovecraft. He took a threatening step toward him.

"You! You were the one who took my—" started R'lsek, then realized he had spoken in the tongue of the humans. "Why am I—"

"Speaking English?" said Lovecraft. "Because it suits me right now. Thought we might have a bit of a palaver. Please, everyone; take a seat."

Everyone in the room took a seat on the various

couches and chairs. Lovecraft remained standing.

"Okay," he started. "Let's cut the crap. None of you are real."

Everyone was speechless. Natty spoke up.

"Would you care to... elaborate a little?"

Lovecraft continued, "I don't mean you're not real as in you don't exist, because you do. By all means. You see, you're basically fictional, created by my imagination. And as such, I have a certain level of control over the happenings of this world." He looked at Zoë. "If not for me, you'd be dead right now."

"How... What was that thing that attacked me?"

"It was a Deep One. They're sort of human-fish hybrids that live off the coast. They're incredibly dangerous, and generally have a taste for human meat. But for genetic reasons, they can't reproduce with each other. They have to do so with humans."

Zoë looked worried. "Wait a minute... you mean that *thing*... it... y'know..."

Lovecraft nodded.

"Then... I'm pregnant?"

Lovecraft nodded.

"With... a *fish baby*," Zoë continued incredulously.

"Indeed. Actually, fish *babies*. You're carrying twins."

"I'm gonna need to sit down."

She did. Or rather, she *collapsed,* her eyes wide

with a combination of confusion and unadulterated horror.

"What do you mean, she would be dead if it wasn't for you?" Natty asked.

R'lsek spoke up this time. "More often than not, Deep Ones, and hybrids thereof, kill their mothers at birth. It's their nature."

"Exactly," Lovecraft said. "But I've altered their instincts a little with my influences. They'll basically be normal human children. Who are fish people."

"Thanks," Zoë said.

"You're welcome. Any more questions?"

"Yeah; why didn't you just stop it before it happened to me?" Zoë looked angry.

Lovecraft had a serious expression on his face for the first time, "I really wish I could have, but it doesn't work that way. I've agreed to follow certain... limitations..." He trailed off, uncertain how to explain further.

Natty raised her hand.

"What do you mean you made us with your imagination?"

Lovecraft looked sheepish.

"Actually, I didn't intend to. You see, my kind have very powerful abilities, and it takes a lot of effort to control them. I'm somewhat of a novice, and I can't fully control them, yet. Suffice to say, I made an oopsie, and I created your world. And yes, I did just say 'oopsie'."

"Your kind?"

"Some call us 'the Old Ones'. But as you can see, we don't seem too old."

"Wait a minute," Natty said. "The Dyer Expedition to Antarctica back in '36 uncovered something they called Old Ones. Claimed they were extraterrestrial."

"Those were a cover-up, actually. An explanation drawn by my subconscious from fictional materials," his gaze fell to the floor. "I'm unfortunately not creative enough to invent a universe on my own."

"Alright, *Old One*," R'lsek said. "Why has the behaviour of the Other Beings changed for the worse?"

"That's my bad. Whenever I make a change, something else changes. The bigger the change, the bigger the reaction. Sort of like the First Law of Thermodynamics. There is no real 'creation' of new material, just a shift from one area to another."

"Can you prove any of this nonsense?" asked Natty.

"Wow. You mean besides the fact that you're all here? You're a hard woman to convince, Miss White. But anyway, if it's *more* proof you want..." He placed his thumb and forefinger to his mouth, blew a shrill whistle.

From the shadows stepped a monster.

It was about five feet tall, head like a Cthulhi (or

rather Cthylha, as it was clearly female, judging by its rope-like dreadlocks), yet more rounded and out of proportion with the rest of its body. Its eyes were immense, and its mouth-tentacles executed in sharp barbs. Its lean limbs ended in digits that had enough joints to be called tentacles.

Cthulhu cocked his scattergun.

R'lsek unsheathed his n'ife.

Zoë scrambled, fell over the couch.

"Hey, hey! Wait a second!!!" said Lovecraft. "Don't shoot, just look!"

Cthulhu and Gray put down their weapons to see that the Cthul-Mi was simply standing still, its awkward shoulders rising and falling as it breathed. Lovecraft put a hand on its shoulder.

"This is Lulu-Gir. She's a Cthulhi/Mi-Go hybrid, but as you can see, she's rather harmless."

Lulu-Gir smiled, raised her hand and gave a small "V-for-victory" sign.

"Okay," said Cthulhu, putting down the scattergun. "We believe you, *Old One*. What we do now?"

"Wait a minute," Zoë piped up from behind the couch. She stood up. "Just because this guy has a freakish-looking pet, you guys are all gonna just buy his line of crap that we're fictional characters? I have a life. I have memories. I'm no more fictional than President Mitchell!"

Lovecraft snickered, but let that one go. He looked

at R'lsek for confirmation.

R'lsek sighed, and his huge shoulders slumped. "First of all, I was conscious when I was transported from Innsmouth to this place; it was an instantaneous conveyance, with a shift in both place and time, and I know of no technology built by *any* of the Races which could do such a thing. Further, the abomination which he controls with such ease not only should not exist; if it did, it would be a ruthless, mindless killing machine. I do not know if I accept his assertion that we are fictional characters, but I must defer to the fact that his powers are unlike anything I have ever encountered, and we do have an invasion on our hands, which must be dealt with."

Zoë shook her head in amazement, unsure what to think, as Natty and Cthulhu appeared to be carefully weighing what R'lsek had said.

Lovecraft nodded. "Alright, to sum it up, there's no need to worry about the hive right now; the Prime answers to me. Gray – sorry, *R'lsek* – will get his weapons back. Zoë, you'll be fine; just get plenty of rest, exercise, and eat your green vegetables. And since Zoë and Gray – I did it again, didn't I? – won't be going home any time soon, I've got two extra apartments right next to mine."

"And where exactly is your apartment?" asked Zoë.

Lovecraft smiled, "Right down the hall. Don't forget to pack a toothbrush. And I'll need to be getting back to it now. Should you need me, you can always come over to my place. The coffee pot's always on, the Internet's free and I've got more DVDs than Gr – *R'lsek''s* body count. See you in the morning, the keys to your respective apartments are on the couch. Goodnight, one and all."

Lovecraft headed out the door, Lulu-Gir close behind.

Natty and Cthulhu looked at Zoë and Gray.

"Well," said Natty, "that was interesting."

DID YOU KNOW?!?!?

"Lovecraft" bears no relation to celebrated horror novelist Howard Philips Lovecraft. He simply chose the name as his moniker because of all the aspects his universe has drawn from Lovecraft's mythos.

XI

In Which Caffeine Fails

==

THRESHOLD ISLAND, FEBRUARY 2

Cthulhu turned the doorknob, and was surprised to find that the door was unlocked. He pushed lightly on the door, as if entering to suddenly would cause him to be struck by some malignant force. The door open, he let himself in. He found himself in the main room of the apartment, which was painted in beige and white. The floors were hardwood, and the walls were sparsely decorated. But the main piece of the room was an enormous flat-panel TV that sat against the wall. It must've measured at least 102 ½". After sufficient awe of the TV, Cthulhu set his sites on his main quarry, which didn't take him too long; in front of the TV was a brown leather couch, and upon that couch was the Coated Man, the Old One – Lovecraft. He was not in his usual attire of a red dress shirt and brown trenchcoat, but black jeans and a battered, hooded sweatshirt. Empty Jolt Cola cans surrounded him.

As Cthulhu moved toward him to try and wake him up, he heard footsteps coming from the vicinity of the kitchen. Cthulhu quickly turned, instinctively unsheathed his n'ife as Lulu-Gir entered.

Cthulhu froze in place as he realized what Lulu-Gir was doing; clutched in one claw and upturned into its mouth was a carton of milk.

Lulu-Gir lowered the carton, wiped its face with its other arm. It noticed Cthulhu and cocked its head quizzically.

"Whodat!" said Lovecraft, bolting upright, Jolt cans clanging noisily to the floor. He groaned, rubbing his temples. "Ugh. No matter how much caffeine you put into your body, it has its limits and eventually gives out."

After clearing his head a bit, Lovecraft looked at the clock. "10:00? Man; never really been up this early."

"Yes," said Cthulhu. "You strike me as the night type."

Lovecraft looked up, looked at Cthulhu as if he had just noticed him. "Hey, Cthulhu. You need somethin'?"

Instead of answering, Cthulhu thrust a newspaper in his general direction. Lovecraft took it, read it aloud, "Strange epidemic spreads. Scientists cannot explain source."

Lovecraft looked up at Lulu-Gir, who shrugged rather human-like. He put the newspaper down, sighed.

"You see," he began groggily. "This is why I can't sleep. When I do, stuff happens that I can't control. You know; 'when the cat's asleep, the mice party down?'"

Cthulhu nodded and logged away that he would have to do everything in his power to keep the Old One awake. Otherwise, he just might have a full scale Mi-Go invasion on his shoulders.

"So, what you going to do about it?" asked Cthulhu.

"Do? Can't really do anything except wait for it to pass, I'm afraid."

"'Pass'? What if it doesn't 'Pass'? The Mi-Go more dangerous than anything. They could destroy Earth."

"If I didn't know that, I would have told you. Besides, I've taken measures. If an outbreak starts, it will be exclusively contained to the island. Believe me; I know what could happen in a full-scale infection. I've been to a universe that –"

He stopped himself, cleared his throat.

Cthulhu understood; an Old One was unable to

reveal much information regarding other realities.

"I understand," said Cthulhu simply.

The Old One was about to say something else, but was interrupted when Gray (they had all agreed to call him Gray, as Lovecraft couldn't seem to keep himself from calling him that) suddenly entered; now dressed in his ominous, tattered black duster.

"I'm sorry," said Gray, in better English than Cthulhu. "Am I interrupting?"

"Not at all," said the Coated Man. "Whaddaya need, Gray?"

"Nothing very important, it's just that Zoë left."

"She... what?" the Old One suddenly looked startled.

"In a taxi, about fifteen minutes ago. We were finished with our weapons training for the day, and she told me that she was going to the hospital to get some tests done. Does that mean anything to you?"

"Oh, bad," said Lovecraft, paling. He jumped up from the couch, sending more Jolt cans to the floor. "Bad, bad, bad!"

"What's wrong?" asked Cthulhu.

The Old One had already moved to the coat rack on the wall, grabbed his trench-coat and his weapon harness, which housed a small, sawed-off shotgun and a dagger. He hurriedly put these items on and addressed his companions; "Lulu-Gir, stay here and hold down the fort. Cthulhu, get Natty. And Gray, for goodness sake, wear a mask!"

Lovecraft hurried to the door, opened it.

"Where we going?" asked Cthulhu.

"To the hospital!" answered the Old One.

==

Zoë had checked into the hospital a half-hour ago, and was now waiting in the imaging suite for one Dr. Hector Munoz, an obstetrician. She didn't know the man, but she didn't really know anybody except for the people she'd been living with for the past month; Natty, Cthulhu, Gray, and Lovecraft.

But that was why she was here; she had been kind of sceptical about what the "Old One" had said a month ago, even though he had made that "Cthul-Mi" appear out of nowhere. So, she decided she'd get some hard evidence. She had to; her abdomen had already noticeably swollen. She didn't have much medical knowledge, but she knew that couldn't be normal – or healthy.

Besides, there was no way she was going to go through an entire pregnancy without seeing a doctor. She should at least be on some kind of vitamins or something. Most of all, though, she wanted to see her babies. She could feel them growing and moving inside of her, and already felt they were so much a part of her, she wanted to be sure of their health, despite their admittedly bizarre origin.

The door opened, and Dr. Munoz entered. He was a younger man of about thirty-two, with blonde hair and an average build. From his tan, it looked as if he didn't spend all of his time as an obstetrician.

"So," he read from his clipboard, his voice a relatively low pitch. "Your iron levels look good; all of your other blood work came back just fine. You appear to be the picture of health. But the bad news, Miss Zoë Allen of Providence, Rhode Island..."

He had spoken her name with a hint of scepticism, as if he didn't quite believe what he had read. "I tried to find your medical records. We couldn't find any such resident of Rhode Island, or of the United States, with your social security number, for that matter."

Zoë paled.

"Is there something you're not telling me, Zoë?"

"No, I..."

"We do have welfare programs for supporting transients—"

"I'm not a *transient*, okay? Do I *look* like I'm homeless?"

"No, but your records—"

"I don't care about my records!" she snapped, "I just want a freaking ultrasound, okay?" Thinking quickly, she took a calming breath, lowered her voice and said, "Look, doctor; I'm paying cash up front for my visit today, and using a false name because I need to keep my private life private. I'm rather glad you don't recognised me, and I'd like to maintain my anonymous status. Are we understanding one another, or does my attorney need to give you a call and give you a tutorial in patient confidentiality?"

Dr. Munoz cleared his throat, straightened his tie, and turned to the ultrasound machine. Zoë leaned back onto the exam table, hoping she'd been sufficiently convincing. As he adjusted the machine, the doctor continued to sneak curious glances toward her as if straining to recognise the girl. Zoë smirked; her assumed cover identity had evidently worked.

Step aside, Michael Westen, she thought smugly.

==

Natty, Cthulhu, Gray, and the Old One walked down the street, rushing through the crowd. It was incredibly cold out, but none of them really noticed.

"I don't understand," said Natty, "What's the rush?"

"We're rushing because Zoë's going to get an ultrasound. And I didn't know about it, which is bad," said the Coated Man.

"And this is bad, why...?"

"Do I really have to remind you what's inside Zoë? If some doctor sees those Deep Ones, they're gonna poke and prod until they find out what those things are, and that's gonna lead back to me. Which can't happen. Not to mention the fact that hybrids are sensitive to ultrasound waves." Then, after a pause, "See, this is what happens when I fall asleep."

"Shouldn't we take a cab?" asked Natty.

"No. We'll get jammed up in the traffic. Walking will be faster. The hospital's only a block away."

"Why are we bringing our weapons?" Cthulhu asked.

Lovecraft looked at him with a strangely enigmatic expression.

"You never can be too careful."

==

The ultrasound machine calibrated, the image started out fuzzy and ambiguous as Dr. Munoz slid the viewing paddle across Zoë's stomach. The ultrasound machine was 3D, so it would give them a fairly definitive image.

When the image cleared, Zoë gasped audibly.

There were two babies, just as the Old One had said, but that wasn't what shocked her; it was the way they looked. They were much too developed for how far along in the pregnancy she was. They looked about six months old, and really didn't look too human; instead of tiny fingers, they had tiny claws. Gills were visible on the sides of their heads. She could've been wrong, but it looked like they already had teeth.

And yet, impossibly, they were absolutely adorable.

"Wow," said Zoë, amazed, placing a hand on either side of her belly.

Her babies. Her children. Her little... Creatures?

"Huh..." choked Dr. Munoz, shocked.

As Munoz moved the ultrasound paddle, one of the babies turned, seemed to look directly at Munoz through the screen, lunged forward.

Zoë saw the skin of her stomach stretch as the baby hybrid attacked the paddle, cracking the plastic housing of the instrument.

The form sank back into her, and she felt the creatures inside her moving. She gently pressed her hands against her stomach.

"Shhh..." She whispered. "It's okay."

"I... um... need to go now," said Munoz, turning for the door.

The exact moment he reached the door, a scream resounded from the hallway.

===

Gray, Natty, Cthulhu and Lovecraft had just

entered the hospital's diagnostic wing when the scream was heard.

Bounding down the hallway was a Mi-Go Infecter.

It could really only be described as a vaguely humanoid entanglement of vine-like growths that constantly undulated with the creature's movements. Its right arm terminated in a long, jagged stinger. It caught sight of the group, screeched. Gray unfurled his razor wire, slung it around the beast's neck. Before Gray could pull the whip and sever its head, the Infecter grabbed the cord, jerked Gray toward it. As Gray was flying through the air, he unsheathed his n'ife, plunged it into its head. He kicked away from the dying creature as it began to twitch with its spasmodic and potentially lethal death-throes. He landed back next to Natty, Cthulhu and the Lovecraft.

"Wow," the Old One said, wide-eyed.

"Alright," Natty said, "Zoë's supposed to be in imaging suite 12."

"And now we have the Mi-Go to deal with," said Gray.

"Shouldn't be much of a problem," said the Coated Man. Behind him, a Byakhee swooped down. The Old One spun, blasted it to steaming bits in mid-air with his shotgun.

"Nice shot," said Cthulhu.

"Thank you."

==

Zoë dashed out of the imaging suite, leaving Munoz to drool on himself. She looked around, saw those accursed Mi-Go mulling here and there.

Well, I wanted proof, she thought, *If only I had a weapon...*

She moved as quietly as she could past the creatures, but she wasn't quiet enough; one of the monsters caught sight of her, screeched. Zoë began to back away, but it leapt at her, pinned her to the floor. It reared back to attack...

...And its head fell off, landing next to Zoë. The body fell backward.

From down the hallway stepped Natty, Cthulhu, Gray, and the Old One. Lovecraft had some sort of device attached to his arm that looked as if it shot bladed disks.

"Come with us if you wanna live," said Lovecraft.

Zoë immediately stood, threw her arms around Lovecraft.

"I'm so sorry I didn't believe you," she said. "And thanks for saving me."

"Um... yeah," Lovecraft said uncomfortably. "Anytime."

When she finally let him go, Lovecraft handed her an arm-mounted sub-repeater from his harness.

Zoë cocked the heavy weapon, pleased that she wasn't helpless, and thrilled that she'd spent at least an hour each day for the past month with one or more of her new companions, working on weapons training.

"Hate to break this up, but we've got company," said Gray, referring to the incoming regiment of about ten Mi-Go Infecters headed down the hall. A hail of lead greeted the first row of them, while some stray Migs that got ahead of the rest were decapitated by Gray's chainsword. One of them managed to get past the lethal rain of death, but was clotheslined by the impossibly strong arm of the Old One.

They finally reached the elevator, and Zoë relentlessly pushed the "down" button.

The scatterguns of Cthulhu and Gray continually blazed, taking chunks out of the monsters but not doing much damage.

"Come *on*!" Zoë screamed at the elevator as the light crawled towards the sixth floor.

"This is getting a little tight!" said Lovecraft.

"Please make elevator go faster," said Cthulhu.

"What do you expect me to do?" snapped Zoë.

Ding!

The doors of the elevator slid open, even as the Infecters stood barely two meters away. The group slid into the cramped space, and just as the doors closed, a Mi-Go shoved its head into the space. Cthulhu hauled back, punched it dead in the face, sending it reeling backwards out of the doors. Cthulhu pulled his hand back, gingerly removing the splinters of the beast's "teeth" from his skin.

They all slumped to the floor, breathing heavily.

"Now, Zoë," said the Old One, "have we learned our lesson?"

Zoë nodded heavily.

"You might wanna explain *this*, though," she said, revealing her distended abdomen.

Suddenly, there was a metallic "THUMP!" from above them, and the ceiling of the elevator began to buckle.

"A little later with that, Zoë," said Lovecraft.

The ceiling split open, the ropey head of a Mi-Go Infecter pushing its way inside, hissing.

Zoë screamed. Natty protectively put her arms around Zoë and they huddled in the corner.

The creature screeched, launching its impossibly long tongue, trying to get at the beings inside the elevator. Gray grabbed the monster's tongue, held it in place.

"*Eat this!*" he screamed, shoved his scattergun against its head, blew its brains out. It shrieked as it backed away out of the hole.

All was quiet, excepting, of course, the tacky elevator Muzak.

===

"That was the scene this afternoon at St. Noden's Hospital on Fourth Street when a major biohazard was contained. Further details are yet to be released, but from what can be gathered, it seems that some sort of chemical spill was involved. The Marines and the National Guard have been called in to help contain the spill..."

The CNN news report played idly on Lovecraft's giant plasma screen. Cthulhu, Natty, Gray, Zoë, and the Old One all sat in the living room of Lovecraft's apartment.

"I believe we've now all learned that when I fall asleep, bad stuff happens. But individually we find that Gray and Cthulhu rock, Natty is good with directions, and Zoë needs to avoid doctors *like the plague*." He took a long draught from his coffee mug. "Are we understood, Zoë?"

"Yes. But about that explanation..."

"Yeah..." Lovecraft looked embarrassed. "I probably should've told you sooner; the gestation period of Deep hybrids is kind of erratic. Sometimes it seems like they're growing incredibly fast, others they seem to not be growing at all."

"Well, that's comforting," Zoë said sarcastically. "So, how am I going to know when they're ready to...

hatch?"

"Well, for starters," Lovecraft replied with that ever-present smirk playing at the corners of his mouth, and his eyes dancing with way too much merriment than the situation warranted. "They don't hatch. You're not going to lay eggs, you know." She looked as though she might injure him, so he hastily continued, "To answer your question, there are certain signs that will indicate that... *hatching*, as you so eloquently put it, is imminent, but you really won't know for sure; you won't have anything like a traditional due date; it could be anywhere within a four to eleven month time period."

"Lovely," Zoë intoned. "So I could be like this for almost a year?"

Lovecraft nodded, then smiled, "On a brighter note, you make excellent coffee."

Zoë couldn't help it; she smiled back. Somehow, in this crazy, impossible situation, she could still smile.

DID YOU KNOW?!?!?

Byakhee bats, while independent organisms, are actually a side effect of overdeveloped Shoggoth growth. Measuring, on average, about three feet end-to-end, Byakhee resemble snakes with bat-like wings and a large, lamprey-like head.

As Shoggoth growth is made up of dead biological matter, thus Byakhee are also made of dead matter.

XII

In Which Movies Are Watched

===

THRESHOLD ISLAND, FEBRUARY 10

Cthulhu, Natty, Gray, Zoë, Lulu-Gir, and the Old One all sat in front of Lovecraft's absurdly large TV. It was about five PM, and it was officially time for movie night to begin. The Old One had one interesting time deciding what movies they could watch, but he finally decided to start with one that wasn't harmful in any way.

"*Alien Monster Chainsaw Horror*?" Cthulhu sceptically asked, looking disturbed at the DVD box he was holding.

"Yup," said Lovecraft, plopping down with a fresh mug of coffee, "It's about a group of teenagers that get locked in a condemned building with a parasitic alien monster."

Gray took the DVD box from Cthulhu, looked in disgust at the cover art, which depicted a disembodied, inhuman head impaled upon a bloody chainsaw.

He simply asked, "Why?"

"Come on, I haven't seen you use your wicked chainsaw sword thingy for weeks, now. I've been jonesing for some raw, visceral chainsaw splatter."

"I'm just guessing here," said Natty. "But I'd venture to say that this isn't exactly a quality film?"

"I wouldn't exactly say quality, but it's generally watchable."

"I guess I'll take your word for it, then."

The Old One smiled, "You don't have to."

He walked over to the DVD player, placed the disk inside of it. The copyright warning appeared. Lovecraft sat down, sinking into the couch, smirking.

"I don't like that look," said Zoë, eyeing him suspiciously.

"Oh, but why?" said the Old One, his voice dripping with sarcasm, "I just can't wait to enjoy this wonderful film."

"This gonna hurt," said Cthulhu.

===

Forty-five minutes later, they were halfway through the movie. On-screen, a teenage boy was busy hacking up the body of one of the aliens, because there were quite a few for some reason. He finished, and he lowered the idling chainsaw. An absurdly attractive teenage girl had been watching him do this, horrified. Her horror increased as she doubled over in pain, grasping her stomach. After a moment of poorly-acted convulsing, a rubber puppet representing an alien burst out of her torso, causing the teenage boy to slash at it with the chainsaw. But it escaped because the fishing line controlling it suddenly retracted.

Natty, Zoë, and Cthulhu were all watching, stunned. Their collective mindset resembled that of a witness to a brutal tragedy; unable to withstand the horror before them, yet also unable to turn away.

Gray wasn't as lucky; he was curled into a ball on the floor, covering his ears whispering the Cthulhi equivalent of "find a happy place."

Cthulhu momentarily snapped out of his reverie to notice that the Coated Man had dozed off, his head drooping to his chest.

"Whoa, uh-oh," said Cthulhu. "Zoë, we've got a caffeine emergency."

Zoë rushed into the kitchen, grabbed a pot of coffee that was always kept on hand for such an occasion as this. She held it up to the Old One's face, and smelling the black liquid, he immediately woke up.

"Whoa, sorry," he said, taking the pot from Zoë. "My defence mechanisms kicked in. My body was protecting itself from harmful agents," he added, gesturing toward the screen. He then downed half the pot with one breath, eliminating any risk of drowsiness.

"I bet Gray wishes he could do that," Cthulhu added, glancing at the now fragile-looking Cthulhi soldier.

"Wait," Natty asked, "Why couldn't he?"

"Gray doesn't sleep."

"Oh. Well, that explains a lot, actually..."

As the movie grew on, Cthulhu began to feel increasingly violated. More limbs flew, and more puppets exploded from stomachs. The movie ended when the chainsaw-wielding boy realized that he, too, was infected, and shot himself in the head. On the sound of the gunshot, the screen blackened and announced "THE END" in bold, tacky letters that resembled dripping blood.

"That's it?" said Gray, now recovered from his trance-state. "I sat through all of that to watch this 'hero' shoot himself?"

"In his defence," said Natty. "I also feel a bit like shooting myself right now."

"Agreed," added Lovecraft. "But then we'd never get to see the sequel."

"Sequel?" Cthulhu said in disbelief. "How you make sequel from that? Everyone's dead."

The Old One said, "Simple. You bring in a completely new cast of characters and have the same exact thing happen to them."

"Clichéd, formulaic, offensive, and *brilliant*," Zoë commented.

"You actually liked it?" Natty asked in disbelief.

"I thought it was an unprecedented masterpiece of unparalleled creativity."

"Really?" Lovecraft said, his sleepy eyes brightening.

"Absolutely. It featured some of the best death scenes *ever*."

"I must admit," Gray said. "The one with the bagel was quite impressive."

"So, who's up for another?" Lovecraft said cheerfully.

"I don't think my brain could take any more," said Gray, rubbing the sides of his head as if against a headache.

"Don't worry," said Lovecraft. "I've got some pretty decent ones."

===

THRESHOLD ISLAND, FEBRUARY 11

It was about four AM. Throughout the night they

had watched several films. Among them were *Screamers*, *Firewalker*, *Omega Man*, and *Night of the Bloodbeast* (Two versions; one was an original Roger Corman film that lasted about an hour, and the second was one that the Old One had concocted himself, which was rather enjoyable). They also watched 1920s version of *The Phantom of the Opera*, simply because it was Zoë's favourite movie and she would've killed Lovecraft if they didn't.

Zoë, Natty, and Lulu-Gir had all fallen asleep, but Gray, Cthulhu, and Lovecraft were still wide-awake. They now sat around the table, playing a friendly game of poker.

Cthulhu was about to win one of Gray's spinblades in a pot that included the Coated Man's dagger, Cthulhu's n'ife, and some 8-track tapes that belonged to Gray, when they suddenly heard a beeping. It didn't take long to trace the sounds to their source: Cthulhu and Gray's personal computers. Gray and Cthulhu immediately opened their computers, looked at them in disbelief.

"Proximity alert," said Gray. "A Cthulhi biosignature has been detected entering the atmosphere."

"Well," Cthulhu said with a shrug, "There's practically a war on, someone was bound to notice."

DID YOU KNOW?!?!?

Alien Monster Chainsaw Horror was made in 2002 on a budget of $50,000. It was written, produced, and directed by exploitation master Finley Woodring (creator of *The Night the Killer Zombies Killed*). He had stated, however, that he was inspired by an idea from actor Bruce Campbell after running into Campbell at a bar in Detroit.

"He said to me, 'I thought it might be cool to hack up those things from *Alien* with a chainsaw'. Then he threw up. Best day ever."

XIII

In Which Love Takes Place

==

THRESHOLD ISLAND, FEBRUARY 15

The Old One walked down the side-walk, casually sipping his Monster energy drink. He preferred Jolt Cola, but Monster was cheaper. Relative pricing of energy drinks wasn't really on his mind though, for despite the fact that it was pouring in thick sheets, he was in a sickeningly good mood. He was, in fact, rather proud of himself; He had essentially saved both Gray and Zoë from certain death. He seemed oddly drawn to people on the brink of death.

He was on his way to the hospital, to check on how the marines and the National Guard were doing with the quarantine. He had used a lot of his strength to destroy all of the Infecters within, but due to annoying restraints, he was unable to effect the larva that may have been inside the patients. Sure, he could alter their biology to make them non-lethal like he'd done for Zoë, but he had no direct influence over their existence. Neither could he get into the hospital to treat the patients with the proper drugs.

The Old One reached his destination, and found that it was still locked tight. Marines guarded the entrance, while the National Guard helped out inside. There would, of course, be no need for the troops; the real threat was already gone. But the government, as Lovecraft had learned, was a glutton for overkill.

Like the days before, there was the usual barnacle-like growth of disaster-watchers, eager to at least get a peek of what was happening inside. But one of them stood out to Lovecraft; she was about five-foot ten, lithe and athletic in build, dressed in crop-top and skirt, with nothing at all to disguise her odd green-hued black skin. From behind the hockey mask she wore came a growth of thick, rope-like dreadlocks.

"Oh," said the Old One.

===

Cthulhu and Gray were suiting up, getting ready for their first mission in weeks for Gray, but months for Cthulhu. They were finishing up, loading advanced shredder shells (containing pellets with small, motorized blades) into their scatterguns.

Zoë and Lulu-Gir both sat on Natty's couch, eating popcorn and watching the 80's version of The Scarlet Pimpernel. Natty, however, was standing by Gray and Cthulhu as they suited up, looking none-too-pleased.

"I don't see why you don't want me to go, Cthulhu. I mean, why do you think you guys chose me to observe?"

"I know, Natty, but I don't want to risk it."

"Come on. It'll be fun."

"Fun, yes. Combat can be entertaining, but *dangerous*."

"And besides," chipped in Gray. "You don't have the proper equipment. No armour. You wouldn't be able to do anything."

"Nobody asked you," snapped Natty.

Gray stepped back once more. *Man, she could get scary*...

"You remember what I did in Arkham?"

She had a point, but Cthulhu still said, "I will not allow you to go without sufficient weapons or armour."

Natty sat down in a chair, defeated.

There was a knock on the door, and Natty answered, a little too snippily, "It's open!"

As Lovecraft entered, his gait more careful than normal, Natty stood and accosted him.

"Hey, Lovecraft, can I fight with Gray and Cthulhu?"

"Don't see why not," said the Old One, not really even paying attention. "I left some equipment on your bed."

Natty smiled like a kid at Christmas, ran to her room.

Lovecraft immediately went to Cthulhu, said, "We have issues. There's—"

But he was immediately cut off by Cthulhu, "You are right that we have issues. Why you give her this permission? You has no right. She not ready to battle this kind of danger. If you were not the Old One, I'd wreak all of the pain and—"

"Wait a minute," Lovecraft smirked that dreadful smirk. "You're falling for Natty."

Cthulhu crossed his arms. "No. That *completely* wrong observation."

"Then why are you defending her irrationally? You know full well what she's capable of."

Cthulhu's embarrassment turned to anger, his death-stare hardening into a doom-stare.

"I defend her because she my responsibility."

"We both know that's a load of bollocks," the Old One became serious. "I've seen those *significant* looks you give each other."

Cthulhu simply looked toward the ceiling. The ceiling did not take objection to this.

"Alright," said Cthulhu, still smouldering. "What is issue?"

"You remember the proximity warning a few days ago, yeah?"

"Yes?"

"The Cthylha that came down… Well, I saw her today."

Cthulhu paled visibly, his complexion matching that of a spoiled oyster.

"Cthylha?"

"Um… Yeah. And she doesn't know that I know, but she kinda followed me home. 'Cause she knew I noticed her. She's probably outside right now. She's fairly street-smart—I think she speaks English."

"*She*?"

"Yes, Cthulhu. *She,*" Lovecraft replied, growing annoyed with Cthulhu's unexplained loss of composure.

Cthulhu's face knotted into a mask of vexation as a dark foreboding overcame him.

There was a knock on the door.

"Come in," said Gray, who was now sitting with Zoë, watching the movie. He tossed a handful of popcorn into his mouth as Jayne Seymour and her big hair filled the TV screen.

The door opened, and from outside stepped the Cthylha in question.

One could only wonder how she slipped about

undetected, despite her flamboyant attire; the hockey mask she wore hid her tentacled face, but was adorned with so many ritualistic Star-Spawn symbols that she looked to be some sort of cultist serial killer. She took off her mask, revealing a face with much larger and more human looking eyes than either Cthulhu or Gray; ice-blue and shining with disconcerting intelligence.

"Hello, E'nasa," she said in perfect English. "You probably weren't expecting me."

Cthulhu blinked, not believing what he was seeing.

"Ja'nis?" He said in disbelief. "Why you here?"

"Lovely to see you, too. I'm here partly for the thrills. I was sailing near Earth when I heard the news of the Mi-Go infestation in a city called Threshold. I was even more eager to come when I found out that you were here."

She was stepping very near Cthulhu, frighteningly intimately, causing him to shy uncomfortably from her.

"Me? Why me?"

"I wish to begin anew," she traced a slender, clawed finger across his face.

He took another dismayed step backwards, shying from her touch. "I thought you wished to never see me again."

Gray and Zoë watched from the couch; The Scarlett Pimpernel had been replaced by something far more entertaining. Gray popped another handful of popcorn in his mouth and handed the bowl to Zoë.

Ja'nis cocked her head, "Why do you say that?"

"I believe it is because of the time you say you never wished to see me again."

"That was just after the battle of Algol, E'nasa. Your grief detached you from your senses; you were gone. You could think of only slaughter and combat."

"I am still in a combat situation."

"Not right now."

She was much too close for comfort, and now her hand was pressed against his chest, from which his heart felt like it was trying to burst. She was very attractive by Cthulhi standards; lean, muscular, the dreadlocks that reached all the way to her waist. But looking at her, all he could see was memories of heartache. She had pledged to be his mate after he returned from Algol, but his unit was decimated; only he and a handful of his troops returned alive. The horrors Cthulhu witnessed racked him with grief, and Ja'nis had left without a word, treating him as though he was not truly worthy of her love.

Cthulhu took Ja'nis by the shoulders, moved her gently away from him.

"Ja'nis, this is too bold of you. You betrayed me, left me to wallow in darkness. And now, you suddenly return, before a mission, asking for my forgiveness? You know I cannot do this."

"I know, but in time, you will share my sentiments. I am sure of this."

At this point, Natty returned from her room, now in full battle-armour. She looked exceedingly fierce, almost robotic. Segmented, plated metal followed the contours of her body, allowing flexibility despite the thickness of the armour. In her claw-gauntleted hands she held a bladed battle-helm.

"Uh, hello?" she ventured, seeing their new guest.

Ja'nis cocked her head, silently appraising Natty. She immediately understood, and looked back at Cthulhu.

"This humen [sic] is your mate?" she said, her tone disproportionately complacent.

Cthulhu's eyes widened, Natty's own expression quickly following suit.

"Back up a bit," she said. "What do you mean 'mate'?"

"'Humen'?" Zoë said, confused at the awkward pronunciation, and wondering just who it was that had just said "sick".

"No, no, no, no, no. No. No. I... Um..." Cthulhu stammered, wishing he was knee-deep in Mi-Go viscera instead of stuck in this disgustingly awkward situation.

"You cannot hide it from me, E'nasa," Ja'nis continued bitterly. "You will not take me back because you already share a life bond with another."

"She... Ja'nis... It's..." Cthulhu struggled to find the right words.

Ja'nis simply turned and walked out the door.

"Well," said Lovecraft. "That was interesting."

"Looks like we have a bit of a soap opera unfolding," said Zoë, a hint of a smile playing across her face.

"What did she mean by 'mate'?" Natty said, her voice cracking.

"I tried to prevent it, Natty," Cthulhu said, embarrassment heavy in his voice, "But I couldn't. I do not even know how it happened; only that it has. Females of my race can see the energy of the life that surrounds us. The sharing of that life energy creates a visible bond, each accepting the other as their mate."

Zoë stood up and said, "I think we need to get over to my apartment and... cook... something."

Gray looked at her, feigning ignorance, "What do you mean?"

She kicked him and he stood up and headed for the door. Just before opening the door, he returned to the couch and got his popcorn bowl. Hugging it to his chest, he headed out the door.

Zoë walked over to Lovecraft, "You're coming, too, Mr. Old One."

"Me? But I think I'm probably needed here..."

She grabbed his hand and hissed, "Do *not* piss off the pregnant girl, God Boy." With that, she dragged him out the door.

"Why didn't you tell me?" Natty said, her voice now a low, soft whisper.

"I couldn't be sure it actually – "

"That's not what I meant," she said, stepping closer to him and touching her hand to the side of his face. "I meant, *why didn't you tell me?*"

Cthulhu, attempting to decipher her meaning, was motionless for a moment. Then, with the realization that she was asking why he hadn't shared his feelings, he hugged her tightly. Natty made no protest to this.

"Because you are stupid humen [sic] girl," he said, his normally raspy voice now soft and low.

She kissed him. Cthulhu had never been kissed before, and he never thought he ever would be. It felt quite unique, and Natty didn't seem to mind the tendrils of his mouth at all. Cthulhu "blushed."

"Don't look now, but I think your allergies are acting up," Natty said with a sly grin. Her green eyes were truly beautiful to him, and he was sure that they rivalled the most exquisite sky ever beheld on his home-world.

Cthulhu trilled softly as he ran a claw through her hair.

After a few moments in which they held each

other, Lovecraft loudly cleared his throat from the doorway. He'd apparently momentarily escaped from Zoë.

"We should go," he said simply.

==

The group assembled outside the apartment, around a manhole that Lovecraft was positive would lead them directly to the source of the Mi-Go infection. The sky was a depressing grey, the laden clouds pouring down upon the city in an equally depressing drizzle. Gray, Cthulhu, Natty, and Lovecraft were now in full battle-armour. Lovecraft had his sawn-off shotgun at the ready, two katana criss-crossed at his back. His right arm was clasped in a sleeve of black steel.

"Alright," said Lovecraft. "Like I told you, we're here to destroy a nest full of a rogue strain of Mi-Go whose Prime I have no influence over. We get in, kill the Prime, get out. Any questions?"

"Yes," came a bitter voice from behind them.

From the shadows stepped Ja'nis. Cthulhu took a step back in an almost ritualistic gesture of bitterness and rejection.

"Is there any room here for an extra player?" said Ja'nis.

She was now decked-out in combat gear; the traditional matte-black plate-metal armour of their equivalent of the marine corps, with some modifications. In her right hand she carried a rather simple but gruesome weapon: a hockey stick with a meat cleaver bolted to the end. The cleaver was sharpened to a razor edge.

"Sure," said Lovecraft. "But you can't use Elder names in this club, sister. Too confusing for us tongue-talkers. From now on, you're... Raven. Got that?"

"Whatever you say, but I'd prefer to choose my own moniker."

"I'd take it if I were you," said Cthulhu distantly. "You're lucky he's even giving you this opportunity."

Lovecraft nodded. "In or out?"

"In. I could use some good sport."

"Good. We could use the help. Are we set?"

Everyone acknowledged their readiness for the task at hand. Gray opened up the manhole cover, revved his chainsword in a final weapons check. Natty slid on the customized battle-helm Lovecraft had given her, and they plunged into the darkness.

They thankfully landed on dry ground, which Natty found to be odd, as this was a storm drain and it was, in fact, raining outside. The thankfulness, however, was short-lived, as Lovecraft lit a road flare, illuminating the room in an eerie orange glow.

The room was covered in chalky, limestone-like sediment; months-old skeletons with exploded torsos appeared to grow out of the walls.

"Shoggoth growth," Lovecraft explained to nobody in particular. "The Mi-Go use it to build their nests and change the atmosphere to suit them better."

"And you're explaining this to us… why?" Natty asked.

"Just call me Mr. Exposition," Lovecraft sneered.

"Let's move along," said Gray.

They moved into a tight tunnel, Lovecraft switching to a fresh flare; he had a whole bandoleer of them strapped to his chest.

They moved into a nursery chamber with hundreds of fresh hosts glued to the walls. They took some time out to cut the hosts down from the walls, but some were too far gone even for Lovecraft to save. They spared them by quickly shooting them in the head. They continued on.

When they reached the adjoining chamber, Lovecraft suddenly paused, cocked his head.

"*Get down!*" He exclaimed as he fired toward ceiling with his shotgun.

An abnormally large Byakhee bat fell from the ceiling, a hole in its face.

Suddenly, Byakhee and Mi-Go poured from facets in the growth, swarming about the group of soldiers.

Immediately, their guns spat loud reports, chain-weapons buzzed, and monsters shrieked.

An Infecter rose up behind Lovecraft, ready to

punch its stinger through his head, but he spun around, jamming his shotgun into its mouth. He proceeded to blow the back of its head off.

It fell backward, its claw slashing down and slicing off half the skin from Lovecraft's face. He gritted his teeth in pain as the flesh grew back in an instant.

Cthulhu grabbed a Mi-Go scout (smaller than Infecters and in possession of large wings) by the throat, stabbed it in the gut with his n'ife before screaming "*Suck wall!*" and then slamming the beast into the side of the tunnel.

Right beside him, Natty cut down numerous Migs with her enormous katana in one hand and a scattergun in the other.

The Cthulhi and the human exchanged a look, smiled. Despite the obstructions to their faces, they each successfully gauged the other's expression.

On the other side of the chamber, Gray watched in wonderment as Raven grabbed a Mig by the throat, head-butted it, threw it to the floor, spun around, smashed down a Byakhee in mid-air with her fist, then whipped back and decapitated yet another Mi-Go with her hockey-blade.

To Gray's own astonishment, this Ja'nis feelings within himself he'd thought long buried. Enamoured with Raven as he was, he fought the disgusting hordes with but half of his brain, but his constant companion, the chainsword, seemed to have a mind of its own and did most of the fighting for him.

Finally, after sufficient gore splattering, the ranks of the Migs and Byakhee had thinned to a few weak, wounded warriors.

Lovecraft walked to one of the wounded Byakhee, put a slug in its brain. He turned it over with his boot, studied it.

"Large body, disproportionate. Means it grew closer to the source," he explained. "The Prime's close."

It was an understatement, of course, seeing as the Prime was literally directly next to them in the adjoining chamber. They found her, weaved to the ceiling to the combination of her Mi-Go tendrils and the Shoggoth growth. At the centre of the mass was a shockingly human figure; an emaciated, skeletal, decidedly female body with a skull-like, eyeless head.

Lovecraft walked up to it, smirked.

"You been a bad girl. And when you're bad, no good can come of it."

The Prime looked down on Lovecraft with contempt; the eyeless gaze attempting to bore into his mind.

"I would not think an Old One such as yourself," it said, its voice liquid and disgusting, "would even think to dirty his hands on the likes of me."

"Well, you glorified foot fungus," Lovecraft smirked over gritted teeth. "You better think again."

With an impossibly high leap, Lovecraft drew both katana from his back, slashed.

He landed, sheathed his blades as the wet sound of the Prime's head falling to the floor resounded. The decapitated, unmoving body was still attached to the ceiling, like some eldrich nightmare captured as a piece of impressionistic art.

Lovecraft turned to the others.

"Our work here is done."

They returned to Natty's apartment, exhausted, their armour scratched and bloodstained. Gray still couldn't keep his eyes off of Raven. Zoë and Lulu-Gir were now watching an episode of the *Immortal Rain* anime.

"Welcome back," said Zoë. "I assume your trip was productive?"

"Yeah, no thanks to you," Lovecraft said in a very sarcastic and mocking tone.

"Being pregnant gives you certain perks," Zoë smiled, patting her stomach.

The overall exhaustion was tempered by Natty and Cthulhu's almost ecstatic joy as they once more embraced one another. By Cthulhi tradition, they were now officially wed. Natty figured there would be no a way to swing a conventional ceremony at this point, so she planned to tell her family that they'd eloped. She didn't mind forgoing the whole poofy dress and walking down the aisle thing; she'd never been much for pomp and circumstance, but maybe they would at least throw a reception...

Raven leaned against the wall, ignorant, possibly intentionally so, of Gray's unwavering (and somewhat disconcerting) stare.

"That was the best slaughter I've had in a while," said Raven.

"Yeah," said Gray, almost sounding intoxicated.

"Hopefully the last one for a while," said Lovecraft.

"Yeah," said Gray.

"I won't be leaving anytime soon, so I'll need a place to stay."

"Yeah," Gray, of course.

"Can I stay here?"

"Nope," Cthulhu said, pointedly averting his gaze. Raven crossed her arms in a visual display of contempt.

"I believe Cthulhu is, well... let's just say 'No Vacancy'," said Lovecraft. "But I believe Gray has some space available at his place."

"Yeah," said... well, you can guess by now.

"I would be honoured to share a residence with an officer, master R'Isek."

"Yeah."

"If I may, I will be retiring now. Good night."

She gave a brief bow of respect, then exited.

"Man," said Zoë. "She's something, isn't she?"

"Yeah."

DID YOU KNOW?!?!?

A rhyme is taught among non-Cthulhi races to help discern the gender of the Star Spawn:

Cthulhi have spikes; Cthylha have dreads, on their heads.

Campy, yes.

Helpful... perhaps.

XIV

In Which Things Are Stolen, and Other Things Are Also Stolen

===

THRESHOLD ISLAND, MARCH 17

"**C**heck mate," Zoë declared as she moved her Queen into position.

Lulu-Gir gave a low, defeated groan, slammed her face on the table, scattering the chess pieces everywhere. They were playing with Lovecraft's special chess board, which he called his "cheese board." It had nothing to do with cheese, but he proclaimed that it was simply a typo, and it had a certain ring to it. They dismissed this as was yet another of his Lovecraftian oddities, and just went along with it.

Zoë looked sympathetically at the Cthul-Mi that

was now practically sobbing.

"Best three out of five?"

Lulu-Gir looked up, nodded. They began to reset the board.

At the other end of the room, Lovecraft was leaning behind his DVD cabinet, over which a sign hung that read "BEST MOVIES IN THE WROLD [sic]! srsly," despite the fact that it housed such movies as *Parts: The Clonus Horror* and *Alien Monster Chainsaw Horror*.

"Screwdriver, please," he called out from behind the cabinet. "I think I see the loose connection."

Cthulhu, standing next to him, handed him the screwdriver.

"Come on, you *piece of* – "

"Where were you on Saturday? I thought we were have another movie night," Cthulhu asked.

"Here, hold onto these," said Lovecraft, holding out a large bundle of tangled wires. Cthulhu obliged. "I kinda had... business to attend to."

"Business?"

"Okay, it wasn't business, it was more like..."

He came out from behind the TV, which was still blurred with static. He bashed the side of the screen once. The start menu for *Dead Space* appeared.

"It was more like 'Alien Monster Chainsaw Horror 2' came out on Saturday, and I really had to be there."

"Uh, huh."

"Yeah. You can ask Zoë. Right Zoë?"

Zoë looked up from her chess game, said, "What was that?"

"You and me went to see *AMCH 2* on Saturday," said Lovecraft.

"Yeah, we did," she said. "It was better than the first one. If you thought the bagel kill was impressive, just wait till you see what Judd Nelson can do with a blender."

Cthulhu's face curled into the Cthulhi equivalent of a raised eyebrow.

"You two is dating?"

"Well, dating isn't quite the word," Lovecraft said dismissively. "What would you call it, Zoë?"

"Dating," she replied.

"Yeah, that's it. We're dating," the Old One said simply. "And we're deeply in love."

"Yep," Zoë said with a pleasant smile directed toward Lovecraft.

"You humens is all insane," Cthulhu said, shaking his head in vexation.

Lovecraft walked fast to the refrigerator, opened it. His eyes widened when he leaned down and grasped only air.

"What the- what the- wha?!," he said, shocked. "All my energy drinks... gone!"

He dropped to his knees, clasped the sides of his

head melodramatically. "I need those to *live*!"

At this time, Gray entered through the door, looking none-too-pleased.

"Hello, Gray," said Cthulhu, over the sobbing of the distraught Old One.

Gray ignored him and headed straight for the chess table, where Zoë had already captured Lulu-Gir's Queen and both Knights. Gray slammed his fist onto the "cheese" table.

"Where are they?" he addressed Zoë angrily.

"Where are what?"

"What do you mean, 'where are what'? You know full well 'what'! The DVDs you stole!"

"...What DVDs?"

"Don't you play dumb! You stole the Charles Dance and Robert Englund versions of *Phantom of the Opera*!"

"You don't understand – "

"I understand perfectly. There's just some pregnant girls that enjoy shamelessly pilfering other people's DVDs."

"No, you *don't understand*. I wouldn't steal your DVDs because I've already got Dance and Englund."

Gray cocked his head, "Then who..."

Raven took this opportunity to barge into the room, bearing a particularly murderous expression on her mask-less face.

"Someone stole my mask. I am not pleased."

Now Natty entered.

"Guys, has anyone seen my laptop --?"

Everyone simultaneously turned to look at her.

"I guess I'm not the only one with a problem."

"There is a thief in our midst," Lovecraft intoned.

==

A floor map of the four apartments was placed onto the table, followed closely by a large mug of coffee. Lovecraft, Zoë, Natty, Cthulhu, Raven, and Gray gathered around the table.

"Alright. Given the close time-frame of the thefts, and the fact that we haven't seen the thief, we can assume he's probably using this system of air vents," Lovecraft said, pointing to a network of tunnels on the map. "We can also assume from the recentness of the thefts that the thief is indeed still in the building; possibly within one of the air vents."

"Okay," said Raven. "Then the best way should be to climb into the vents and flush him out."

"We can't all go in," said Natty. "There needs to be a guard for each of the vent exits to catch the thief as soon as they exit the vent."

"I'll go," said Lovecraft. "I'm small enough to fit in the vents."

"Hey, I'm not *that* pregnant," Zoë said. "Why shouldn't I go?"

"We don't know what we're up against. Could be dangerous. And factoring in your... condition, I don't want to take the risk."

"There's still me," Natty said. "Are you implying something about *my* size?"

Lovecraft stared at her, vibrating with confusion for a moment, stumbling over which words to use and then threw his hands up to eye level. "Listen, *I* am going. Simply because *I* am *volunteering*. Is that okay with everyone?"

They all affirmed this.

"Alright. Raven can take my apartment; Natty and Zoë can take her apartment, Cthulhu can take his and Natty's, and Gray can cover his own. Any questions?"

Silence.

"Good. Dismissed."

==

"Alright," said Lovecraft, his voice echoing slightly within the cramped shaft. "I'm in."

"Okay," Zoë's voice came over his radio. "The first intersection is about three meters ahead. Go down one level and turn right."

He continued for three meters and came to a drop. As he climbed the ladder, he said, "I find it only fair to warn you that I'm slightly claustrophobic. If you hear me whimpering and crying, just yell at me to snap out of it and I'll be fine."

"Will do."

Lovecraft reached the next level and turned right.

"Alright, I'm in the tunnel."

"Head forward another meter. According to the map, there's an emergency maintenance hatch to your left. It'll lead into a large storage compartment. That's the most likely place he'll be hiding."

Lovecraft opened the hatch, shone his LED torch within just to see a pair of legs disappear into another passage above.

He dashed in, shining his torch into the small hole.

"He's escaped into a ceiling hatch."

"That leads into the next tunnel. There should be a hatch to the adjoining passage in front of you."

He opened the hatch, the figure of the thief dashing past him. He grasped at the fleeing figure to no avail.

"Man, he's fast!"

He briefly noted the various stolen items crammed into the storage space, then watched as the thief headed toward the exit of the tunnel.

"Zoë, he's headed right for you!"

===

Without warning, the vent grate burst open,

liberating a small boy in tattered clothes. Natty caught the figure in a constricting bear hug, the boy's shaggy blond hair flying about as he thrashed against Natty's grasp.

"Just a little boy..." said Zoë.

"*Ouch!*" exclaimed Natty as she felt a sudden pain in her hand. She immediately dropped the boy, examining her hand; the boy had bit her.

The boy ran and hid underneath a coffee table.

Lovecraft climbed out of the vent, neatly landing on his feet.

"Where is he?"

Zoë pointed. "Underneath the coffee table."

Lovecraft started toward the coffee table, where he now could see the figure of a little boy crouching underneath it.

"Careful," said Natty, nursing her wounded hand. "He bites."

Lovecraft lifted an eyebrow at the absurdity of the statement. He continued his approach toward the cowering figure underneath the table.

"It's alright," he said, his tone gentle. "No one's gonna hurt you."

He finally arrived at the table, crouched down. His eyes widened in shocked recognition as he saw the face of the little boy.

"Who are you? Where's Mr. Persei?"

==

"Joseph 'Joey' Slater. Born January 12, 1901 in Catskill, New York. You're about six years old."

"Yeah," said the boy, sitting on Lovecraft's couch. Zoë had gotten him a mug of hot cocoa.

"You were admitted to a psychiatric hospital at age five because of your bizarre dreams, and your tendency to act violently in your sleep. Your doctor was named George Kyle Persei, and he was the only one who knew about your abilities."

"How do you know so much about me?"

"I can't exactly explain *how*– "

"He's your guardian angel, sweetie," said Zoë, sitting down next to the boy.

Lovecraft shot her a dirty look, but decided to follow along, "Yeah, sure. You could think of me that way."

Joey looked at Zoë, directed an oddly concerned stare towards her stomach.

"You have monsters in your tummy," he intoned.

Zoë's eyes widened, and she stood up.

"How do you – "

"I just know, is all."

"Joey here has a different type of perception from you and I," Lovecraft explained. "He has an added sense that allows him to discern and understand the existence of Other Beings. Unfortunately, this also made him a conduit for... other forces."

"They're not gonna hurt you, right?" Joey asked Zoë.

"No, they're not, honey."

Lovecraft said, "They're not like the things you've seen in your dreams, Joey. They're... good monsters."

"Okay."

Lulu-Gir took this opportunity to enter the room, munching on a package of Gummi Savers.

Joey caught sight of her, screamed, jumping into Zoë's arms.

Lulu-Gir also screamed, ducking underneath a table, covering her head.

"It's okay, it's okay!" said Zoë, trying to calm Joey down.

"Look," said Lovecraft softly, approaching the cowering Cthul-Mi. He placed his hand on Lulu-Gir's head, patting it gently, as much reassuring Lulu-Gir as he was Joey. Lulu-Gir slowly emerged from underneath the table, sitting on all fours. "See? She's nice."

Joey looked uncertainly at Zoë, who nodded, putting him down. The boy cautiously approached the Cthul-Mi.

"Go ahead. It's okay."

He reached out, put his hand on the soft skin of Lulu-Gir's head. The Cthul-Mi began to purr happily. Joey smiled cautiously.

"See? She likes you."

Joey laughed joyously when Lulu-Gir licked her own eyeball. With the boy preoccupied, Lovecraft walked over and joined the others.

"What we going to do with him?" asked Cthulhu.

"Well," said Lovecraft. "He seems to have taken a shine to you, Zoë. Maybe he can stay with you."

"I'm not sure I should, Craft," Zoë said.

"Come on, Zoë. You'll do great."

"You're just saying that."

"Yes," Lovecraft smiled. "Yes I am. Besides, you need the practice."

Zoë sighed in feigned annoyance.

"I guess I could give it a *try*..." She said, her voice heavily coloured with sarcasm.

DID YOU KNOW?!?!?

Dr. George K. Persei's studies on Joey Slater's mental state eventually led to the advent of shared dreaming technology. This technology is used today, in moderation, to diagnose and treat mental disorders. It is incredibly risky, however, as sharing a dream with a mentally disturbed individual may lead to inadvertently absorbing certain aspects of their condition.

XV

In Which Cthulhu Attends a Comic Book Convention

==

THRESHOLD ISLAND, APRIL 3

(Lovecraft's Mind)

Morning.

The hunt.

Not really used to being up this early. My friends insisted.

The sun is just beginning to show its bright face in the horizon.

Leaping across the rooftops. My knees scrape in the gravel. I wince, but pay no real heed; the skin will grow back.

The concrete jungle.

Threshold is my territory. My home.

I catch movement to my right.

I turn, but the figure is already gone.

...Slippery fish.

Movement. Left. Gone in an instant. I spin, catch sight of my quarry. He raises his n'ife.

Sloppy, my friend.

In a single, fluid motion, I slice his n'ife in half with my katana; grasp the much larger warrior by the throat, hoisting him off his feet.

"Game over, friend."

Suddenly, cold steel is pressed to my throat.

===

"Game over, Craft," Raven said. She lowered her hockey blade, taking a bit of care not to slice open Lovecraft's neck.

"I hate it when she does that," he mused to himself. "I didn't know you were out here."

"First rule of the field: expect everything."

"Sure. Never heard that one," he said acerbically. Then added, "Got anything about 'expect your opponent to cheat'?"

"You're being a sore loser," Gray said. "And

besides, you're an Old One. You could, I don't know, smote us down with lightning or something."

Lovecraft groaned, "For the last time; I'm not God!"

===

Zoë and Joey walked down the street, carrying armfuls of bags. Zoë had taken the boy shopping for new clothes, and they'd already visited about fifteen different stores.

"So," Zoë asked, "Where do you want to go next?"

Joey itched his shoulder through his black t-shirt.

"These clothes feel weird."

"I'm sure clothes were quite a bit different a hundred years ago. You'll get used to them."

Joey suddenly got a strange, distant look on his face as he stopped. Zoë noticed this, walked over to him. She knelt to Joey's level.

"What's wrong?"

"I really have to get back to the hospital," Joey said, concerned, "Mr. Persei, he's wantin' to do some tests on my brain and stuff. He gets real worried when he can't find me."

"Joey, you can't go back to the hospital. I'm sure Mr. Persei knows you're safe, anyway."

"No, I don't think so. Mr. Persei, he said there was this thing, this thing in my mind. Somthin' about being 'open to external influences'. He said he needed to fix my brain so the things couldn't get into it."

Zoë smiled, "Lovecraft's already taken care of that for you, Joey. You might say he's... somewhat of a brain specialist."

Joey laughed and hugged her.

"Now," Zoë said, straightening. "Let's get back to the apartment. I'm sure Lovecraft needs me to make more coffee."

As they were walking, Zoë suddenly noticed a public bulletin board that she had seen before. She smiled broadly as she noticed one bulletin in particular.

==

(Cthulhu's Mind)

I *hate computers. They are a roundabout, overcomplicated method of sending and receiving information. Speech. Radio. Phone.*

All immensely simpler, all immensely preferable.

The web of information called "teh internets [sic]" is, for lack of a better term, evil. It has a nasty habit of throwing images at you that you have never wished in your life to see, it leads you down dark, endless paths of nonsensical advertisement (which, in itself, is evil), and it will lie to you constantly.

I look across the "page" before me: ALIEN MONSTERS ON THE LOOSE? And a very roughly drawn sketch of me, Gray, and Raven.

Gray has mandibles.

I have a Mi-Go skull on a spear.

Only it is long, smooth, has no eyes, looks biomechanical.

And it's on the Weekly World News site.

Our secret remains safe.

I click over to some real news; ALIEN MONSTER CHAINSAW HORROR III IN THE MAKING?!

I am already pondering ways to hide this

information from Lovecraft.

==

Natty was making a fresh pot of coffee. Lovecraft had just returned from training with Gray and Raven, and he was dangerously close to falling asleep. Natty silently prayed that her coffee proved to be as caffeine-heavy as Zoë's (even if it was, he would still prefer Zoë. Biased little freak).

Lovecraft took the mug she offered gratefully and took a sip.

"I'm just saying it ain't fair to team up on me without telling me."

"You're still being a sore loser?" said Raven. "Get over it."

"Yeah. You're acting like a noob," agreed Gray. He agreed with Raven quite often.

"You're just lucky I didn't have my powers on full blast."

Zoë took this opportunity to enter through the door unannounced, Joey in close tow. She wore an enormous grin.

"You look particularly giddy today," said Lovecraft. "What's goin' on?"

"Oh, nothing," she said sarcastically. "I just... won *eight first-class round-trip tickets to PwnCon in Finley!*"

Lovecraft's eyes widened, "PwnCon!?"

"PwnCon," Zoë said.

Gray repeated, "PwnCon?"

"What that?" Asked Cthulhu.

Lovecraft turned to him, "One of the best and unique comic conventions in the world. It's like nirvana for geeks. And I seriously just called myself a geek," he added, grimacing.

"I've got enough tickets for everybody," Zoë smiled. "So, who wants to come?"

Seven hands rose simultaneously.

==

JOSEA PICKMAN AIRPORT, THRESHOLD ISLAND, APRIL 13

Cthulhu growled a strong barrage of Elder Tongue curses as he stared down an old enemy.

The escalator (of DOOOOOM!!)

Cthulhu knew he shouldn't be afraid of things so... mundane in the human lifestyle, but he wished this cursed thing would just die.

He took one cautious step forward, then quickly followed with his other foot. He trilled proudly to himself as he ascended. He finally reached the top, found solid footing, and raised his fist in silent triumph.

When he snapped out of his reverie, he noticed his seven companions regarding him with annoyed expressions.

"What?"

"What took you so long?" asked Zoë. "We've been waiting up here for like fifteen minutes."

"I think our little E'nasa has a phobia he didn't tell us about," said Raven smugly.

Lovecraft snorted, suppressing a laugh.

"It isn't funny! The escalator's scarry [sic]!"

===

"How are we gonna get into the terminal?" asked Natty. "If you haven't noticed, we look kinda... conspicuous."

Lovecraft smiled. "I prepared for that. All of you who aren't human, go ahead and close your eyes, and don't open them till I say so."

Cthulhu closed his eyes tightly, and he felt a tingling sensation fill his body. It abruptly stopped when he heard Lovecraft say;

"Alright, you can open them."

The first thing Cthulhu noticed when he opened his eyes was that he was about a whole foot shorter. He still loomed over Lovecraft, Natty, Zoë and Joey, but...

His hands!

Soft... short nails... pink skin...

He was human.

He ran over to a window, looking at his reflection. It was unlike anything he could have imagined.

He had chiselled features, a slightly pointed nose (he had a nose!), green eyes, brown, spiky hair. The effect was mildly disquieting, and he quickly lifted his transformed hand to his new face in a bizarre combination of shock and glee.

Suddenly, Gray and Raven were next to him, wearing similar expressions, inspecting themselves.

He almost didn't recognize them, but in a strange way, their new appearances... suited them.

Gray was much older than him (Cthulhu looked like he was in his twenties, while Gray looked about forty-five), with a rounder head, buzz-cut grey hair and a matching goatee. Raven was much shorter than both of them (about 5'6"), around twenty, black hair with purple highlights, and blue eyes.

They eyed themselves and each other, shocked. They looked back at Lovecraft, who smiled.

"It's only temporary... just until we get to Finley. Y'know, so nobody cries 'terrorist'."

Without warning, Natty practically tackled Cthulhu, planting a kiss on Cthulhu's previously non-existent set of lips.

When she finally released him, she said, "Wow. That was a bit different."

Cthulhu simply nodded his agreement, still in shock over both what had just taken place and the sensation that had accompanied it.

"Not better, mind you," she continued, smiling. "Just different."

Cthulhu smiled back at her. With his *mouth*. He held a hand up to his lips, which were tingling, and then took her hand in his.

They now noticed Lulu-Gir; she was now a girl of about fifteen, with blonde hair braided into dreadlocks. Her bright yellow t-shirt was tucked into faded blue jeans, the tattered hems of which hung over her worn-looking black and white chequered hi-top Converse All Stars. She sat on all fours next to Lovecraft, licking his hand.

"Rowr," she said.

==

They were now headed for their gate, and it was a lot easier going now that the escalator was past, even though there were many more people.

Cthulhu liked the moving side-walk a bit more than the escalator, but it still got a black mark on his mental list of human objects.

But Joey loved it.

His forward momentum combined with the motion of the side-walk in an effect that rendered to him inhuman speed reminiscent of the Flash.

As Cthulhu, Natty, Zoë, Lulu-Gir, Gray and Raven simply rode it, he would continually barge past them, get off, run to the back, and get back on again. Obviously, such riotously fun objects such as this did not exist in the early 1900s.

They got off the side-walk and looked at the flight schedule; the flight to Finley was to depart at twelve noon.

Gray looked at the clock. It was only ten AM. In unison, the group groaned in annoyance.

"What are we do until then?" asked Cthulhu.

"Find a book store?" suggested Raven.

"Wander the terminal?" Gray.

"Ride the side-walk?" Joey.

"Sit down?" Zoë.

"Rowr?" Well... you can guess.

"Well," Lovecraft said, staring wide-eyed past them. "I think I've got something we can all agree on..."

He pointed behind them, and they all turned, saw what he was looking at.

A Grounded!™ Coffee House, glimmering as if it were a celestial body.

"It's... beautiful..." said Lovecraft, tears in his eyes.

==

Most of their time at Grounded!™ was rather uneventful, but passable. Natty took advantage of the coffee shop's wireless internet, while the rest enjoyed the coffee and told stories. Zoë stood outside the shop and supervised Joey on the sidewalk, until she convinced the boy to stop and come into Grounded!™, where she bought him a hot cocoa. The only real incident was around eleven forty, when Lulu-Gir suddenly jumped over the counter and began frantically eating coffee beans.

"Please excuse my sister," Lovecraft attempted to explain. "She has... dementia."

"Rowr," Lulu-Gir contributed.

This excuse was insufficient to keep them from being kicked out of the coffee shop.

However, the next twenty minutes passed mercifully quick, and the plane began to board.

==

"You sure this is safe?" Cthulhu said nervously.

Natty changed positions uncomfortably as she attempted to relieve the pain of Cthulhu's grip on her hand. But she was mostly used to it. Mostly.

"Yes, Cthulhu, I'm sure. What're you worried about? You've flown in space, without anything surrounding you. How can this be worse?"

Cthulhu looked around himself, his eyes wide with

fear.

"Because," he said. "That's what Cthulhi do. This is *technology*. Humen [sic] technology. It's different."

"You're saying you've got a problem with human technology?"

In earnest, he had no trust for human technology, but didn't want to appear rude. "No, it's just..."

"You're saying you distrust humans in general?"

"No. Humens [sic] is fine."

"Then why should you worry?"

Cthulhu sighed, and his shoulders dropped, only for them to tense back up when the plane started to move, the flight attendant's voice reminding them to make sure their tray tables were up and their seat backs in the full, upright position.

"We're gonna die..." said Cthulhu nervously. "We're gonna *die!*"

"We're not going to die, Cthulhu. We're just flying."

"That's why we're gonna die."

"Cthulhu, we're safe. We're in the air. Please let go of my hand?"

Cthulhu looked around. "We're flying... We're flying!!"

He laughed nervously, then frowned, realizing the implications of that statement. He jumped from his seat, smashing his head against the ceiling, then running down the aisle, screaming.

He stopped when a flight attendant suddenly appeared out of nowhere, stopping him dead in his tracks.

"Sir, I'm going to have to ask you to return to your seat. You're frightening the other passengers."

Cthulhu seemed to shrink by several feet as he returned to Natty and sat down, his eyes still wide with terror.

"It's okay, Cthulhu," said Natty. "It's gonna be alright. Gray and Raven seem fine."

Gray was sitting in the seat across from them, reading a magazine. Next to him, Raven casually turned the magazine right side up, as Gray had been "reading" it upside down. She then resumed the reading of her book.

A few seats back, Zoë, Lovecraft, Joey, and Lulu-Gir all sat in the same row. Lovecraft was enjoying a fresh cup of coffee as Lulu-Gir practically vibrated in her seat (I guess the only thing worse than a Cthul-Mi in human form is a Cthul-Mi in human form with ADD).

"Rowr," she said impatiently.

"Lulu-Gir, please," said Lovecraft. "I've got a lot to do before we get to PwnCon."

"Rowr..." she replied disappointedly.

She began to read a magazine, but her attention was immediately stolen as the drink cart wheeled by. Before the stewardess knew what was going on,

Lulu-Gir jumped onto the cart, throwing her arms in the air with a cry of delight.

Lovecraft buried his face in his hands.

"What did I do to deserve this?"

"Everything," Zoë snickered, playfully elbowing him in the ribs.

===

They made it to Finley alive, despite the constant warnings of impending doom that Cthulhu constantly muttered.

They took a cab from the airport to their hotel, where they checked in and dropped off their baggage. From there, they made their way to PwnCon.

They stepped out of the cab, now in their natural forms, sans masks or disguises, and headed toward the large building that establishment that hosted this year's PwnCon.

"Now remember, guys," Lovecraft told them. "Once we get inside, just act casual. There's no need to be on the defensive here, and when we get inside, you'll see why."

They made their way to the entrance, which, Cthulhu noted, seemed to be a magnet for Trekkies; he could've sworn that he saw at least five Spocks and around two-dozen Kirks.

After a short wait in line, they came to the man admitting them in; he was sturdily built man of about thirty, who was comfortably dressed as Han Solo with a short, brown coat and a DC-17 blaster secured at his hip.

"Tickets, please?"

"We got a group of eight, here," said Lovecraft, handing him the tickets.

The doorman stared wide-eyed as the guests filed past him. Though in civilian clothes, Gray, Cthulhu and Raven looked exceedingly imposing.

"Nice costumes, huh?" said Natty, walking past. "We've been working on 'em for months."

===

PwnCon was taking place in a very large hotel and the adjoining mall, with the main events occurring in the huge atrium at the centre of the mall (out of which branched the five wings of the mall, giving the establishment a vague star shape). Their hotel was on the outskirts of Finley, as every hotel within a sanely reasonable distance of the event had been booked for weeks in advance.

Situated at various places in the atrium were stands and kiosks of every imaginable variety. Lovecraft took notice of one particular kiosk that was surrounded by a large group of people wearing long, brown coats.

"Excuse me, ladies and gentlemen," he said, moving past them toward the kiosk. "This is my stop."

He reached the crowd, and was greeted warmly. Cthulhu could not make out any conversation, but he heard several shouts of acknowledgement, and various phrases in an unknown language.

"What're you guys supposed to be?" Cthulhu heard a voice say from somewhere to his side.

He turned, and found a boy of about nineteen, with light-blonde hair and shadowed eyes. He wore a oddly-styled scientist's smock that was draped loosely across his wiry frame. As he spoke, he did not face Cthulhu, but instead looked forward, at something seemingly very interesting, that only he could see.

"Are you aliens or something?"

"That is one way of putting it," Gray intoned.

"Fascinating. My name is West," he said, extending his hand. However, his eyes remained averted. It was oddly unsettling, as he was obviously not blind; he'd addressed them, and commented on their group's appearance, and yet he had done nothing but look dramatically off into the middle distance. Natty ignored the urge to line her head up with his to try to discern what he was staring at.

"Cthulhu," Cthulhu shook his hand perfunctorily,

and dropped it quickly, as if slightly unnerved by the boy. And with good reason; his hand felt like a dead haddock. "And these are my associates, Gray and Raven."

Raven seemed to take some slight offence at being called his "associate."

"Nice to meet you. Well, I gotta get going. I've got things to do."

West turned, disappeared into the crowd.

"There was something strange about him," said Gray.

"He would not look at me," Cthulhu said, staring at where West had disappeared to.

"Guys," Lovecraft shouted, running up to them. "You wouldn't believe who I just saw!"

He paused, thought, "Well, I guess you would believe it, since you've never heard of him."

"Who was it?" asked Natty.

"A particular person who's not even supposed to be in this world. I guess, you know, he fits in this world, but it should be *him*. Not like this... This guy Charles Dex --"

The lights abruptly failed, cutting him off.

When the lights came back on a second later, someone immediately screamed bloody murder. The room erupted into unintelligible conversation as everybody crowded simultaneously away from and toward the source of the scream.

Shoving through the crowd, the group of Cthulhi and humans tried to make their way toward where everybody was looking.

When they finally reached the centre of the teeming crowd, what they saw was both a shock and not surprising at the same time (it can happen); kneeling on the floor was a teenage girl dressed in a Star Wars shirt with an Ewok on it. She clutched her arm in pain, as a small but visible Mi-Go stinger protruded from it, drawing a trickle of already coagulating blood.

Cthulhu, Natty, Gray, Raven and Zoë simultaneously looked at Lovecraft.

"Don't look at me!"

"Then who...?" Cthulhu said.

At the other end of the room, West stood in the shadows, smirking. His eyes blinked, turning a dead, cataractic white .

"Now the fun begins."

DID YOU KNOW?!?!?

Charles Dexter Ward was once a well known chemist who turned to the ways of "dark alchemy". He discovered that he could, in fact, absorb the agility of others by distilling their spinal fluid and injecting it into his own spine. Initially using donors for his experiments, he eventually lost his sanity in a blind thirst for power, and resorted to hunting down live human sources. He is now partially reformed, working as a sort of paranormal mercenary. His incredible agility lends a major advantage in this occupation.

XVI

In Which Things are Explained, and a Plan is Laid

==

FINNLEY, ARIZONA, APRIL 14

(Natty's Mind)

Okay, this is how it feels to be me right now.

I'm married to a Star-Spawn, for starters.

That's a weird statement in and of itself.

Next, I find out that we're going on what seems to be an actual vacation. But lo and behold, some really freakish crap decides to start happening.

Now this vacation is becoming another combat op.

And it's not any normal op.

Lovecraft says that there might be other, more

dangerous beings involved.

And someone just as powerful as him. Maybe more so.

And this guy's got some real malicious intent.

So here I sit at the edge of a hotel bed, discussing what to do about it with four monsters (one of whom is my husband), a pregnant teenager, and an inter-dimensional spaz while a deeply disturbed six year old boy sleeps soundly nearby.

==

"Do you think it's another Old One?" asked Zoë worriedly.

"It has to be. There's nothing else that could suddenly generate a Mi-Go stinger spontaneously in the middle of a crowd. And counteract my power," the Coated Man replied, taking a drink of his Monster. He frowned. "None of the others would want to do that, though," His voice trailed off, and none of them heard him say, "It can't be *him*..."

"How is the girl?" asked Gray.

"She'll be fine. She was in the beginning stages of infection, so I just gave her an injection of pseudoethereal acid. It should dissolve any developing embryos."

"Has she been taken to a hospital yet?" asked

Natty.

"About that. All communications—cellphone, landlines, internet—are completely blocked off. Aside from these few blocks around PwnCon, we have no contact with the outside world."

"We can still go to get help though, right?" said Natty.

"No. It acts as a physical barrier as well. Observe."

He walked over to the window, drew the curtains back. They all looked out the window to see what appeared to be a normal cityscape—that stretched several blocks, but just suddenly ended in inky blackness.

"What is this?" Gray said in disbelief.

"Ambiguity Barrier," explained Lovecraft. "Nothing gets in or out. It's as if neither side exists to the other."

"So," said Zoë. "What do we do?"

"We stop him. If we apprehend him, everything he has done can be contained."

"Only problem is," Cthulhu said. "We don't know where he is or even *who* he is."

At that moment, they heard a knock on the door. Lovecraft removed his shotgun from the holster on his back, slowly moved toward the door, looked out the peep-hole. His wary look was soon replaced with a pleased smile as he opened the door. Behind the door was a boy of about Lovecraft's age, only slightly shorter, with blue eyes and a mop of messy, blue-dyed hair, wearing a black t-shirt emblazoned with silver Elder symbols.

"Carter!" shouted Lovecraft, catching the blue-eyed kid in a bear hug.

"Good to see you too, Lovecraft."

"What're you doing here?"

"Heard you were at PwnCon. Decided to drop over, catch some of the action."

"You might've bit off more than you can chew in that department."

"Excuse me," said Natty, annoyed. "I hate to break up this emotional reunion, but *who are you?*"

"Guys," said Lovecraft. "This is Randy Carter. He's another of the Old Ones," he turned to Carter. "Carter, this is Natty, Cthulhu, Zoë, Gray, and Raven. The sleeping boy over there is Joey."

"A pleasure."

"Now, Carter," Lovecraft said, his tone darkening. "About all this weird stuff happening. Please tell me it's not *you* behind it all."

"I wish it was; then we'd have a bit less to worry about. Actually, Lovecraft, it's West."

"West," Cthulhu echoed, recognizing the name.

"West's here?" said Lovecraft. His voice betrayed urgency and... fear?

"I thought he was dead. Executed by his own creations."

"Didn't we all. But he's survived somehow. I tracked him here on a tip from a reliable source. The creation of this new universe of yours was quite convenient for him, Craft."

"West is an Old One?" asked Cthulhu.

Carter and Lovecraft looked at him.

"You know West?" said Carter.

"I just met him at PwnCon. I knew there was something strange about him..."

"He was creepy," Gray intoned.

"No," Lovecraft said. "He's not an Old One. Though he sure would like to be. He's just a greatly disturbed young man who discovered a hallucinogenic substance that allowed him to transport his mind and body to alternate realities."

"Once he found out that he had influence over these realities," explained Carter. "He got creative. He invented and refined a compound that could resurrect dead tissue. Specifically human."

Lovecraft added, "He destroyed the entire world in one reality. Actuated a zombie apocalypse."

"How much influence over this world does he have?" Cthulhu asked. "I mean, he is only humen [sic], not Old One."

"Actually," Davis explained ruefully. "His weird, twisted logic and morbidly creative intellect give him even more influence than us. Given a week, he will have raised enough soldiers to drown this reality in its own blood."

"So, how do we stop him?" Zoë asked.

"What about you, Raven?" Gray asked the Cthylha "You've been less than verbose."

Raven shook her head as if snapping out of a reverie, "Hmm? Oh, I dunno. I just kinda got stuck on the whole zombie apocalypse thing. Sounds fun."

Cthulhu rolled his eyes.

"Actually," Carter interjected. "I took the liberty of bringing along my entourage."

Carter opened the door, and from the hallway entered three young boys of about twelve. They were all identical, with their pale skin and lanky, almost emaciated physiques, but each wore a different expression; the first's eyes blazed with an otherworldly darkness, the second carried a mischievous grin, and the third simply looked indifferent.

"May I introduce to you Nug, Yeb and Aphoom," Carter introduced the boys respectively.

"To disperse any ambiguity," Nug said. "I am the god of fear. Y'know, the visceral kind you get when you're in a dark alley, and you've no idea what lies in the dark." He grinned evilly. "That's me."

He looked directly at Gray, who cringed in fear, "Unfortunately for you, I do not represent the mortal fear to which you are immune. That's reserved for our cousin, Dalen."

He gestured to the boys next to him, "These are my brothers. We are triplets, and I am convinced I have been cursed with them as my eternal punishment for my very nature."

"I just break stuff," Yeb said. "I don't get paid to play nice."

"He's the god of chaos," Aphoom said, putting a hand on top of his brother's head. "And he's quite good at it. Nug and I pale in comparison to his wondrous might."

"Nice job on the sarcasm, Aphoom."

"It's my job."

"Pleasure to meet you," Cthulhu said. He added, "I think," under his breath.

"Great to be here," said Nug. "Makes a nice relief from my normal job."

"Here, here," Yeb agreed. "Sowing fear and chaos is entertaining, but after a while, it can get *boring*."

Aphoom intoned, "You want boring? Try filing people's responses under 'monotone' and 'tongue in cheek'."

"Guys," Carter stopped them, "Let's not start this stuff again."

"Sorry," the triplets said in unison.

"So, do we have a plan?" asked Natty.

"Get to PwnCon," said Nug.

"Find West," intoned Aphoom.

"Do what we do best," said Yeb.

"Oh," Carter said. "There's one more thing."

===

They stepped into the cool night air, (which was odd, because it was 10 AM, and it was freaking Arizona), and only then did they realize the scope of the Ambiguity Barrier; it blocked out everything, to an extent that it was big *onto the sun*. It seemed as though they were floating on an island in the middle of an infinite black abyss. Once they had gotten used to the Dark Wall (which wasn't easy), one thing was immediately prevalent: a huge, singed Armoured Personnel Carrier parked next to the curb, sitting on its haunches like a olive-drab, armoured toad.

"Ooh," Lovecraft squeaked. Gravitating toward the vehicle, "Niiice ride." Shaking himself out of his dazed stupor, he added, "How come you get an APC? All I got was a rusty Dodge Dynasty."

"Dude, I love that car!" Carter replied.

"Wanna trade?"

"No."

"Interesting," Raven said.

"Well, what're we waiting for?" Lovecraft said jubilantly, climbing up into the vehicle. "Let's see what this puppy can do!"

As soon as he had entered the APC, a high-pitched scream issued forth as Lovecraft stumbled backwards out of the vehicle, landing flat on his tush.

"Badbadbad!" He stammered.

"What's the matter, *Old One*?" came an evenly calm, ominous voice. A figure dressed in simple dress slacks and a white shirt with a black tie stepped out. "An entity of your stature should know better than to fear corporeal death."

"Ward, this isn't you, man! You're not supposed to be... serial killer... ish."

"Relax," said a disembodied voice. "In this universe, Mister Charles Dexter Ward may be a psychotic killer, but he's a psychotic killer on *our* side. Specifically under my employ."

"Wait," Lovecraft said, standing. "That voice..."

A figure now emerged from the shadows; that of a girl around 18 years old, dressed in a deep purple t-shirt and blue jeans. What was unusual, however, was that her skin and hair were both pure ivory. Her eyes were a disconcerting shade of pure black.

Lovecraft smiled, "Lavinia. It's been a long time."

"Yes," Lavinia said. "It has."

She walked up to him and gave him a warm hug.

"Lavinia Whateley," Carter stepped up. "Looking... pale and creepy as always."

"Why, thank you, Randy," Lavinia said pleasantly.

Lovecraft said, "I guess you were Carter's source?"

"No. Ward was, actually. He seemed quite

enthusiastic about the prospect of ruining a fellow lunatic."

She turned to Ward and said, "No offence."

"None taken," Ward gave a small bow in her direction.

Lovecraft said, "Did you come by yourself?"

"Not at all."

From the shadows stepped a huge, imposing figure. He was a man, to be sure, or possibly a magic-spawned golem; for he was about seven feet tall and three feet thick. He wore an ebony mask that closely resembled a skull.

"Hey, Anton!" Lovecraft said, stepping toward the giant figure. "How you doin' with the whole bodyguard thing?"

The giant man lifted his right arm, extended his thumb from his massive fist.

"I'll bet it didn't take much convincing to get you here."

Anton shook his head.

Off to the side, the others watched on with fascination.

Natty turned to Carter, said, "Lavinia is an Old One, isn't she?"

"Yeah, she is."

"And who is big man Anton with ebony mask?" asked Cthulhu.

"He's Lavinia's personal guard. Don't really know

too much about him, only that Lav recruited him in some other universe, and he's been with her ever since."

"That's kind of ambiguous," Zoë remarked.

"That's all I know."

"Ahem," Ward cleared his throat. "I hate to interrupt, but West is most likely literally raising the dead as we speak."

"An excellent point, but we have to pick someone up first," said Lavinia.

"Who?" asked Carter.

Lavinia got a strange, smug look on her face.

Carter paled, "No. Not her."

==

At the corner of Kleiner and Breen St, the APC stopped and the door opened. Waiting there was a group that looked most definitely out of place. Standing on giant, tree trunk-sized legs was a creature that looked to be the love-child of a yeti and an elephant. Large, ram-like horns protruded from the sides of its head, atop which rode a small girl of about sixteen years. She slid down from the beast and deftly landed on her feet.

"Good boy, Azathoth," she said to the beast; said beast responded with a deep "huff".

The group in the APC waited while Lavinia got out

and greeted the newcomer enthusiastically.

"I'm so glad you could make it, Bas," said the Old One.

"Wouldn't miss it for the world."

"And you brought Az!"

She strode over to the enormous beast, scratched behind his ear.

"What has Bas been feeding you, boy? Last time a saw you, you were no bigger than a Dalethe spore!"

Azathoth replied with a pleased huff.

Lavinia then turned toward Bas, her face stern.

"You got the sit-rep file?"

Bas nodded, held up the folder she'd been carrying. It was labelled simply "212."

"Looks pretty bad," she said. "Serious energy spikes over the past few days, and not just from the Ambiguity Barrier. West's got something big in store."

Lavinia nodded. "We'll be ready."

"Don't be so sure."

The others, not privy to the conversation between the two girls, waited at the APC.

"You're going to have to greet her at some point," Lovecraft said to Carter, who was curled in a ball in the corner of the vehicle. "Might as well get it out of the way."

Carter merely babbled something about "gagging with a spoon."

"Is he alright?" asked Cthulhu.

"Yeah, just ignore him," replied Lovecraft.

Zoë said, "So, I guess this is the part were I ask who *those two* are."

"More Old Ones?" guessed Cthulhu.

"No," Lovecraft said, "She's actually... well, she's the goddess of..."

Lovecraft lapsed into an embarrassed silence.

"The goddess of what?" Natty asked, annoyed.

"She's the goddess of... cuteness."

Zoë made a choked snorting sound, indicating suppressed laughter.

Cthulhu, for the first time, noted Bas' appearance; innocent, petite, soft features, a tail and ears that fit better on a big cat rather than a human figure. As she moved, she seemed in possession of a kind of self-contradicting "clumsy grace." Just looking at her, Cthulhu felt the overwhelming urge to hug her.

"Should it really surprise you?" Aphoom said, "If there's a god of sarcasm, why shouldn't there be a goddess of cuteness?"

"Actually I'm still trying to get around the idea of a 'sarcasm god,'" Natty said.

Zoë, recovering from her quiet laughter, said, "Next you'll tell us there's a god of... cake, or something."

"Yes, but Gladys and I haven't spoken in three years," said Aphoom. "She's a pathological liar."

"She's not the only one," Yeb muttered. Aphoom nudged him in the ribs. He nudged Aphoom in the ribs. Aphoom nudged him harder. Yeb punched Aphoom in the head, collapsing him.

"Come on, guys," Nug said. "We don't want a repeat of Monday."

Lavinia and Bas were still conversing, so Lovecraft put two fingers in his mouth and let out a shrill whistle, gathering their attention.

"I hate to interrupt girl time, but... psychopathic doctor; Ambiguity Barrier; evil?"

Bas looked speculatively at the APC.

"Will we all fit?"

"Don't worry," Lovecraft said with a grin. "It's bigger on the inside."

Indeed it was. In fact, it was several meters in volume, and resembled the interior of a cargo plane, aside from the presence of a pinball machine, an air hockey table, and a Mountain Dew machine.

Closing the door after her entourage, Bas' face suddenly brightened; she'd spotted Carter.

"Oh, crap," said the Old One.

Before he could manage another word, the young goddess was upon him, catching him in what will be referred to as an "epic glomp."

"Carter, I can't believe you made it!"

"Yeah, good to see you, too, Bas..." Carter returned, turning an unhealthy shade of purple. "I...

can't... breathe..."

Natty turned to Lavinia, "Do they... um... know each other?"

"What was your first clue?"

===

(Zoë's Mind)

Watching Bas' reaction to Carter, I can't help but wonder if there's some sort of underlying force that individually governs each Old One.

Perhaps for Lovecraft it's lack of sleep.

For Lavinia, maybe Lovecraft himself.

And for Carter, there's Bas.

For each impossible power, there's another power to balance it out. I find myself more and more hopeful about this suicide mission we're sending ourselves into. We now have a virtual army of Other Beings; despite how awkward everybody acts, Anton exudes quiet confidence, or perhaps indifference. Azathoth is also quite formidable. Add to that mine and everybody else's previous battle experience...

In my laypersons opinion, a force that is not to be screwed with. As the APC slows in front of the PwnCon buildings, we get out, and armour is dished out. This time I get a scattergun and a satchel full of shells, and I'm more confident than ever.

But as we head through the front door, I feel something...bad.

DID YOU KNOW*?!?!?*

PwnCon has run for three consecutive years. It has quickly grown into one of the most well-known comic book conventions on the continent. It is known for hosting the largest collection of replica firearms of any exhibition in the world.

XVII

In Which War Is Waged

==

FINNLEY, ARIZONA, APRIL 14

(Gray's Mind)

It's high noon right now, but you wouldn't know it from the inky blackness that surrounds the city.

I can't say I ever expected to find myself in a scenario of this kind; impossible happenings, battling not for patriotism or sport, but to defend my friends... who aren't even all of my Race.

We're now at the PwnCon site, performing a final weapon's check.

Carter dons a suit of mechanized battle-armour, which makes him easily as tall as me. Of course, armour isn't everything. But it helps.

Various projectile weapons are handed out, along with blades of varying shapes and sizes.

"How is this going to play out?" I ask.

Lovecraft hefts a generous-sized, chain gun-like weapon.

"Loud."

We make our way toward the main building, when Zoë doubles over, dropping her scattergun.

I have a bad feeling about this.

===

"Zoë, are you alright?" asked Gray.

Lovecraft hurried to her side.

"I'm fine," she replied, picking up her scattergun. "Just a stitch."

Lovecraft looked at her quizzically, but she annoyedly reiterated that she was fine.

"Alrighty," Bas said. "But what about *that*?"

Bas pointed toward the hotel. Up until this point, their focus had been on the mall. They now noticed that the entirety of the building was sheathed in a chalky, mineral growth. Shoggoth growth.

"Well, that's not good," Lavinia said.

Cthulhu asked, "What we going to do about it?"

Carter smiled, patted the side of his APC. "Leave that up to me."

"Alright, here's how this is gonna work," Lovecraft said. "Lavinia, Cthulhu, Raven, Ward; you all come with me and Carter. Gray will take Zoë, Natty, the triplets, Azathoth, Bas, Joey, and secure the mall."

"You got it," Gray said, racking three rounds into his scattergun. "Triplets, you reconnoitre, and meet me in the main atrium in eight minutes."

Aphoom gave him a crisp salute, accompanied by a smirk. Nug and Yeb followed suit. Yeb gave a backward-handed navy salute, but after being elbowed by Nug, changed it to a flat army salute.

"Wait, wait, wait!" Natty was holding one hand up, flagging them down. Everyone stopped and stared at her. "Haven't any of you been paying attention to all of the movies that we watch? Aren't we making the number one horror flick mistake? Splitting up our forces. Hello?"

Lovecraft smiled, "You know, Natty; you have a very good point." He paused for effect. "However, we have to split our forces because there are two distinct missions; one: find West, and two: keep the PwnCon attendees safe. That's actually why we have so much help; we're not actually splitting our forces; we're combining four sets of forces into two teams. See? Aren't I brilliant?"

"Yeah, I'm all aflutter," Carter said. "Bad guy to fight; innocents to protect now, okay?" He turned back toward the hotel.

Bas jumped onto Azathoth's back and proceeded toward the mall. Lovecraft grabbed Gray's arm.

"Gray, take care of her," he said, looking toward Zoë.

Gray nodded, turned toward the mall.

"Right," Lovecraft said to Carter. "Let's do this."

==

In a spray of white fragments and masonry, the APC burst through the wall of the hotel.

Coughing on the plumes of dust, Carter stepped out, proclaimed, "That was *wicked*."

"Too bad we didn't have high-speed cameras set up," Lavinia said. "It would've looked like a Michael Bay movie."

The rest of the team climbed out of the vehicle, lastly Lovecraft, who made a gagging sound at the mention of Michael Bay.

"Would you look at that," he said, pointing to the doorway that was spaced a good six feet from the hole. "Missed by *that much*."

"It was a decent enough attempt," Lavinia said.

"Decent?" Carter was offended. "That was near perfect, considering I had no idea I was even aiming for the door."

"Gentlemen," Ward called to them.

Without so much as a sound, he had made his way

to the staircase that led up to the higher rooms; it was coated in the same growth as the outside of the building.

"Is this problem?" Cthulhu asked.

"No," Lovecraft said. "Not at all. It might be a trap, or West might be somewhere in here. Either way, we climb."

===

Gray kicked open the main door, (which was unnecessary, as it was already open) brandishing his scattergun. Behind him, Azathoth barged in, followed by the others.

Instead of insectile shrieks or the moans of the undead, they were greeted by an uproarious wave of cheering and applause.

Sweeping the area with his gaze, Gray saw not the enemy, but hordes of comic book fans.

"Well," Gray said. "This is certainly awkward."

"I think they're cheering for you, Az," Bas said.

Azathoth looked toward the crowd of fans, smiled (which looked more like he was trying to dislodge something stuck in his teeth). The fans cheered louder.

Bas beamed from her perch and favoured the crowd with her best "princess wave."

"This is just wrong," Gray said, starting toward the

crowd.

"Don't we merit applause?" Yeb said, disappointed.

"What makes you think they even know who we are?" Aphoom said.

"Are you kidding?" Yeb said. "I have an enormous fan base. Complete with fangirls."

"Mmmmm... fangirls..." Aphoom said whimsically.

"I believe I gave you imbeciles an assignment," Gray growled.

"Don't get your ridiculous plate metal combat armour in a bunch," Yeb said. "If we're going on a possible suicide mission, we're gonna bloody well make it a fun one!"

The triplets turned as one and hurried into the crowd.

"Are you sure you're alright?" Natty asked Zoë. The girl was desperately trying to mask her pain.

"Yeah. I'm good; I just need to sit down."

Natty looked sceptically at the girl, but said, "I'll get you some water."

"Thanks," Zoë said, sitting down on a bench.

Joey took her hand and said, "You are really not well right now." He climbed onto the bench next to her and snuggled up tight, putting his hand on her bulging belly.

Zoë had noticed that her babies had gone through a recent growth spurt, but she had no idea it was anything serious...

Gray accosted an attendee, who happened to be dressed as Isaac Clarke from *Dead Space*, and demanded, "What is going on here?"

"What's it look like? We're enjoying the convention."

Gray realized now from the attendee's voice that said attendee was female – he couldn't tell through the bulky armour and helmet. She then said, "You guys are all *totally awesome*. Can I touch your tentacles?"

Gray shied back, suddenly uncomfortable. He said, "No! What's the matter with you all? Did you not notice the obviously preternatural goings on?"

The Isaac Girl scoffed, "Duh, of course I've noticed. Look around, man. This rocks, especially when you compare this to my job at Grounded!™. I mean, did you see that big black nothing outside?"

Another attendee dressed as some sort of vigilante said, "Word. This is the best con *ever*!"

Gray sighed, "This is gonna be a long day."

==

On the staircase, in the hotel, things were less annoying. They were, however, no less challenging.

"Are we there yet?" asked Lovecraft, exhausted.

They'd been climbing the spiral staircase for near

half an hour.

"Not yet," Ward replied.

"I think we're in the... teens, somewhere," Lavinia said.

"Tell me when we get to twenty," Lovecraft gasped, "I'm gonna throw up."

Ward took a significant step away from Lovecraft.

"Seriously, are we on escalator or something?" Cthulhu said. "We don't seem to be getting anywhere."

"I'm starting to think it might be a possibility," Carter said.

They continued their trudge up the stairs, nothing but staircase in sight.

Then, they saw nothing.

"Wassat?" Lovecraft's voice said.

"Power's been shut off," Cthulhu said. "Apparently West has a few other things in store for us."

"Hold on a sec," Lovecraft said.

A second later, a road flare lit up, illuminating the staircase in a flickering red glow.

And revealing a drooling, ropey face.

==

"How's it going?" Natty asked Gray. He was sitting on the edge of a particularly pleasant-looking fountain at the centre of the atrium.

"Not good," the Cthulhi replied, "The major disadvantage to defending a bunch of geeks from monsters is that geeks think being attacked by monsters is 'awesome.'"

"What're we gonna do about it?"

"Nobody's going anywhere, and West obviously hasn't launched an attack on this place yet, so I say we lay low and wait it out."

"Sounds good."

At that moment, Yeb came up to them and plopped a rather large stack of comic books on the fountain's ledge.

Gray pointed at the stack, "What're those?"

"Comic books."

"I can see that. What're you doing with them?"

"I'm... reading them?"

"No, no you're *not* reading them."

"Why not?"

"Because we're here on serious business. We need to remain focused and alert. You were supposed to be pulling recon. Where are your brothers?"

"Don't know," Yeb crossed his arms, pouting. "And don't really care."

Gray stood to leave, but his foot slipped on a turtle that wasn't there a second ago. He fell backward, splashing into the fountain.

"Did I do that?" Yeb said with a cheeky grin, "Oopsie."

Gray growled at him.

Natty rolled her eyes, stood.

"I'm gonna go check on Zoë."

She left. Gray began wringing the water from his duster.

"Look on the bright side," Yeb said, reading a comic. "We could be stuck in an elevator."

Gray kicked water at him.

"Dude! That is *so* immature!"

==

Zoë was having a hard time keeping it together. The pain was getting considerably worse, and the sweat on her brow was sure to betray her emotional struggle.

I'm only four months along, she thought to herself. *I don't care what Craft says; I can't possibly be in labour...*

Joey had been sitting next to her the whole time, and she'd completely forgotten. The boy looked very concerned.

"I'm okay," she told him, annoyed at how strained her voice sounded.

"I don't think so," he said, leaning against her again. "I think Mr. Craft needs to help your babies like he helped my brain."

Natty was now standing behind the bench, her

scattergun slung on her back. She leaned on the back of the bench, said to Joey, "Joey, go make sure Gray isn't killing Yeb, okay?"

Joey opened his mouth to protest, but decided to simply comply. As soon as he was out of earshot, Natty said, "Zoë, you're clearly not alright. If something's going on with you, we can't have it compromising the mission."

Zoë looked reluctant, but after a while said, "Okay, ever since we got here, I've been having these cramps. They're pretty bad, and I think I might be..."

"Might be what?" Natty said after Zoë's reluctant pause.

"I think they might be contractions."

"Oh, crap."

Zoë suddenly doubled over, groaning with pain.

"They're getting worse," she said, her voice strained.

"Lovecraft won't like this," Natty said, pulling out her cell.

==

Lovecraft, frozen, dropped the flare he had just lit. The suddenly-revealed ropey face belonged to a Mi-Go Infecter, one that didn't seem too keen on the idea of letting Lovecraft and his crew past.

It opened its mouth, its barbed tongue poised to

strike. Lovecraft closed his eyes...

But the blow didn't come.

Lovecraft slowly opened his eyes, and saw the barb of the tongue a good inch from his face. Holding onto the tongue was Anton's impossibly huge hand. The golem looked at Lovecraft, nodded.

The Infecter screeched, slashed down on Anton's arm. As the blow connected, the tongue came off in the Anton's hand, but the monster didn't seem to register the pain. It reared up to strike Anton, but was blown backward by a blast from Raven's scattergun.

"Did you seriously lock up like a frightened horror movie girl?" Cthulhu said.

"Not sure how to reply to that."

"The correct reply would be, 'Yes, yes I did, Cthulhu. Thanks for saving my hide, Anton,'" Lavinia smirked.

As the rest of the team piled onto the writhing monster, Lovecraft's ring tone sounded (a punk rock version of *Non, Je Ne Regrette Rien*). He removed his phone from his back pocket and said, "Lovecraft here."

"Hey, Lovecraft. It's Natty."

"How're things over at the mall?"

"For the most part, boring. But we've kinda got a situation."

"What kind of a situation?"

"I think Zoë's in labour."

Lovecraft nearly dropped the phone, but maintained his composure. "Are you sure?"

"No, that's why I called you."

"Alright, there's some – "

He was cut off when the Infecter gurgled/screeched as its arm was cut off. Covering the receiver of the phone, Lovecraft said to either the warriors or the Infecter (or both), "Do you *mind*?"

The gurgling was cut off when Ward cut the beast's throat with a razor blade.

"Thank you. Now, as I was saying, there's some indicators you can look for."

"Like what?"

"Well, are the contractions evenly spaced?"

"Yes."

"Well, that's not a definite way of telling... Is she feeling strong movement from the babies?"

"Yeah."

"Crap. Still not definite, though. Let's see... what else... Oh, yeah! Have her eyes changed colour?"

"What? No... her eyes are still grey."

"Alright. Tell her she's not in labour."

There was silence for a moment; Natty was probably giving Zoë the news.

"She wants to know how you can tell," was the reply.

"The parent's eyes always change colours during labour with a hybrid. Sometimes red, sometimes yellow, sometimes iridescent plaid. It depends on the species, but there's always a discernible change."

"That's very interesting, but what is really going on with her?"

"Over extended growth spurt. It's fairly common in these instances, and it can be quite painful, but not harmful unless she overdoes it. She shouldn't strain herself at all."

"Shouldn't strain herself?" Natty sounded incredulous. "We might be about to head into battle at any moment and she shouldn't strain herself? How is *that* gonna work?"

"Look, the others should be able to pick up the slack; find the safest place you can for Zoë to wait it out with Joey. Also, I left three tablets of lambdathol in your ammo satchel. Have her take them with a full glass of water. That should calm her babies down. Until then, please keep her out of trouble."

A pause.

"Are you an ethereal being or a doctor?"

"Here I'm a doctor, but that's just because I've invented most of the medications and their accompanying ailments."

"I'm gotta get going now. I'm sure you have an evil mastermind to find and disable, and I've got a pregnant teenager and a little boy to take care of while preparing for war against the undead."

"Thanks."

Lovecraft hung up. He noticed that the Infecter was now a pile of bleeding, dismembered limbs.

"Go team," he said, genuinely impressed.

"We try," Lavinia said.

"Well, we've got a long way to – "

Lovecraft stopped mid sentence.

He suddenly felt warm and cold at the same time. A numbness permeated his chest.

He looked down, saw the Infecter's tongue barb protruding from his sternum. It had acted independently to stab him through the back.

"Huh...?" the Old One breathed.

As he slumped in pain, everyone rushed over to the fallen Old One, who was now creating a wide, crimson puddle on the floor. Lavinia pulled the writhing tentacle out of Lovecraft's back, tossed it to the side.

"Torch it!" she yelled to Carter, who let out a burst from his incinerator. The tongue shrivelled like overcooked bacon.

"I'll be f-fine," Lovecraft said, his voice weak. "I'll be fixed up in a few. Just t-takes a little l-longer for the b-big stuff."

"Are you sure?" Raven asked.

"He'll be fine," Lavinia said. "Takes more than a little knick like that to keep an Old One down, right

Craft?"

He smiled faintly, "You know it, Lavinia." He was polite enough not to mention the tears shining in her eyes. In truth, this was a more serious injury than any he'd ever known an Old One to obtain in a universe of his own creation. They were usually pretty well taken care of with their incredible regeneration rates, but West was changing all of the rules...

"Lovecraft," Cthulhu said. "We can't do this without you."

"Sure you can, Cthulhu. I have every faith that you guys are gonna noob-slap that sissy West. I know I couldn't have picked a finer team of weird, fictional characters to hang out with," he coughed some blood. "So, get to it. I'll stay here; I just need a little sleep."

As his eyes closed and he curled into a foetal ball, the rest of the group reluctantly turned down the hallway.

"Trust me. He'll be fine," Carter reiterated.

"I just hope *we'll* be enough to win this thing," Cthulhu said, taking point.

Going into a situation such as this, however, Cthulhu couldn't help feeling a little pessimistic. West had practically the entire observable world under his thumb, and he had even managed to disable one of the only people capable of defeating him. But hey, it's not like he he'd never faced impossible odds.

It was practically in his job description.

===

"What do you mean I can't help?"

Natty had to physically hold Zoë down on the bench to keep her from reaching her scattergun. She had willingly taken the lambdathol pills, but only before Natty informed her that she wouldn't be doing any fighting.

"Lovecraft said that you can't strain yourself until the babies calm down."

"But, Natty, I fight – " she winced in pain, then continued, "I fight fine. It's just pulling a trigger."

"No means no. He loves you, Zoë, and he wants what's best for you. He said that you and the babies will be fine as long as you don't strain yourself right now. Besides, it would probably be best for Joey if you kept him with you if things start getting ugly."

Grudgingly, Zoë lay down on the bench.

Natty turned and approached Bas, Azathoth, and Nug, who had just returned from their patrol.

"We've finished our perimeter sweep," Nug said. "No sign of anything unusual. Unless you count two Trekkies dressed as Chekhov and Uhura making out."

"That's disturbing," Natty said.

"You have no idea," Bas replied with a shudder. "I need some brain bleach."

"West will make his move here," Gray said, coming up behind Natty. "I can feel it. I can feel it like it's..."

Suddenly, they noticed slurping sounds that seemed in very close proximity. They all looked down and saw an emaciated, pale, dead-looking man chewing on Gray's armoured foot.

"...attached to my boot."

Suddenly, a horde of undead flesh eaters poured out of nowhere and dog piled onto Gray.

The rest of the group reached for their weapons, but before any of them could get off a shot, a shrill buzzing sounded, and Gray's chainsword emerged from the pile, swung, and the zombies flew off him in varied states of dismemberment.

"If that was all," Natty said. "I'm gonna be quite disappointed."

A loud moaning drew their attention to the other end of the atrium, where a legion of the dead were gathered, loping toward them with hunger in their eyes.

"Careful what you wish for," Bas said to Natty.

===

"*West!*" Cthulhu called out, his voice booming and intimidating. At the very top of the stairs, they were led down a long corridor that led to a single mahogany door. They had opened this door to find an enormous room that could not have possibly been contained within the hotel. It echoed eerily with sounds of dripping water and creaking.

"Lookie here at who decided to show up."

The voice came from a distant corner of the room, where shadows blanketed the floor. The odd group of warriors all drew their various weapons.

"Given you guys' track record, I am sorely disappointed in how long I've had to wait."

The shadows seemed to gather, mould, grow out of the floor, until they formed into the shape of a long, white smock. West stepped forth to greet them.

"My, my, what an odd looking bunch. All except you, Lavinia; you look more lovely each time I see you."

Lavinia growled deep in her throat, a murderous gleam in her dead-black eyes.

"You'll pay for what you've done," she said.

"You hurt Lovecraft you little --"

Cthulhu raised his n'ife and rammed it right through West's heart.

West's eyes went wide as he gasped, but the gasp immediately gave way to a sly smirk.

"Tisk, tisk, Cthulhu."

He pulled himself away from the blade, the silver

now stained totally with red.

"Trying to kill the discoverer of the secret to immortality?" he said. "Shame on you for this uncharacteristic show of ignorance."

"You haven't gained immortality," Carter said. "Fake immortality, maybe."

"Oh, I believe this is all quite real, my old friend. So real, I think we'll be taking permanent residence here."

"Wait," Raven said. "'We'?"

"Oh, I forgot," West said in his annoyingly pleasant monotone. "You haven't met my new ladyfriend. Say hello to the boys, dear."

A new figure emerged from the shadows; skeletal, but plainly female. Ropey, eyeless, a lipless mouth housing needle-like teeth.

The Mi-Go Prime.

"Hello, Cthulhu. Raven," the Prime said, its voice clearer and more human than previously.

"You..." Cthulhu said. "How?"

"It's amazing what one can do when one truly puts their mind to it," West said. "When I escaped to your little universe, I saw how cruel you'd been to you'd been to poor Prime, here. I just had to help."

"After he brought me back, West and I realized we had a common motivation," the Prime explained. "Revenge. I on Lovecraft and his little private army, and he on the Old Ones in whole."

West continued, "So everything works out. We'll get to kill all of you, and set up camp in this universe. Once we've raised a nicely sized family, with the help of the Other Beings Lovecraft so kindly enraged, we'll wage war on the pathetic Old Ones, eventually taking all pseudo-realities as our own."

"I love it when you talk cosmic domination, Westy," the Prime breathed.

West grabbed the Prime and pulled her close. His mouth found her lipless face. Suddenly, they were making out.

"Brain stamp," Carter groaned, making a retching sound.

"That is easily the most disgusting thing I've ever seen," Ward grimaced.

"That was a very nice villain rant," Lavinia said as the two strange beings parted. "But answer me just *one* more thing."

"Go ahead," West said, one arm slung over the shoulders of his "ladyfriend."

"How much will you enjoy cosmic domination with one frigging eye?"

In a blur of motion, a razor blade left Ward's hand and embedded itself in West's left eye.

==

The undead horde was slowly advancing, and the

team was having a difficult time holding them at bay, even with a constant wall of lead being laid down. Azathoth was lifting up attendees and depositing them on the above balcony, which had been sealed off as a fall-back point that was now cut off.

"This isn't working," Natty said, the chain of ammo being quickly eaten by her sub-repeater. "They don't die when you shoot them in the head!"

"Dismembering them seems to work," Gray said. "Aim for their limbs."

One of the undead vaulted over their ranks, somehow insanely agile. When it landed, however, it was crushed to gooey bonemeal by Azathoth's fist.

"*Owned!*" Bas shouted.

The guests, along with Zoë and Joey, had now all been evacuated to the balcony. With the constant ammunition discharge, the hordes were dwindling two a manageable "bunch." However, it was at this exact moment that Aphoom fired the last round from his minigun.

The last few dozen zombies drew near, and the group prepared their blades.

They suddenly heard a hollow "thoom!" and a grenade rolled at the zombies' feet. After a split second, the explosive detonated, sending zombie parts flying every which way.

They all turned to the balcony to see Zoë wielding a sub-repeater, its grenade launcher barrel steaming.

"I got better," she smirked, using a hint of a British accent.

They turned back towards the north-east wing of the mall, where another bout of moaning was beginning to resonate.

"You guys ready to rock?" Zoë said with a gleeful smile as she tossed them some replica firearms that had been miraculously rendered not-so-fake.

"'A transfer of material.'" Gray quoted the Old One.

===

West removed the razor blade from his eye, uttering a foul sequence of obscenities that didn't even fit together. He covered the mess with his hand, blood spewing from between his fingers.

The Prime's sockets widened as she screeched with horrified shock.

From the growth-covered ceiling, a swarm of Byakhee descended. Carter swept his incinerator in a wide arc over their heads, and a number of the bats fell to the floor, charred.

While they were distracted, the Prime took the opportunity to run headlong into Cthulhu, slashing at him viciously with her claws, letting out a feral gurgle-shriek.

The others were too preoccupied fending off the

Byakhee to help him. Through the cloud of leathery wings and teeth, they could see West, sneering behind the blood on his face.

The Prime had knocked Cthulhu to the floor, straddling him and stabbing him with her razor-pointed knees at the same time. She made an attempt at biting into Cthulhu's tentacles, but the Cthulhi grabbed her face, rolled, planted a knee on the Mi-Go's ribcage. He slowly pressed down, the wood-like bones snapping loudly. He leaned down, removing his n'ife from its scabbard.

"*West!*" the Prime screamed. "*Help me!!*"

West simply remained behind the wall of Byakhee, smug in his annoying cowardice.

The Prime looked up into Cthulhu's death-scowl. The blade came down.

"Not again."

Her head rolled from her body, the Prime's shocked expression still frozen on her disembodied face.

The Byakhee screeched, but their attacks became more insistent.

"This isn't right," Carter said, his breathing becoming laboured. "With the Prime dead, the Byakhee should've dispersed."

"She wasn't who was controlling them," Lavinia said, looking toward West.

Anton, holding off several Byakhee with his bare

hands, looked at Lavinia. Lavinia looked back, nodded. Anton lowered his arms, began to march directly into the swarm.

"What you *doing*?" Cthulhu said, shocked.

"Don't worry," Lavinia said. "He's been waiting for this a long time."

The Byakhee gnawed relentlessly at Anton, sometimes taking bits of his body, but the pain did not matter. What mattered was fate.

Having made it through the maelstrom, Anton brushed the few stray Byakhee from his coat. He looked directly at West.

"What... How?" West said, his eye wide with shock.

Anton stepped forward.

"Stop! Don't come any closer!"

He didn't stop.

"Do you have any idea *who I am*?" the psychopath whined.

Anton was now directly in front of West, mere feet away. He removed his ebony mask, revealing a warped, broken, dead-looking face under a bald scalp.

"I do," he said, his voice raspy, gravely, and Michael Clarke Duncan-esque at the same time. "*Father.*"

===

MISKATONIC UNIVERSITY, MASSACHUSETTS, PSEUDO-REALITY PR-117

MANY YEARS AGO

West stood, trembling. His hand went limp, and the syringe fell from it, clattering to the floor. Before him stood a behemoth of a man; incredibly tall, incredibly powerful, incredibly angry. Just three minutes ago, this man had been dead from natural causes; a heart attack resulting from his disproportionate physiology.

The injection had returned life to him, but because of the manner of his death, Anton would, even in his immortality, constantly feel the pain of death.

The brownish, naked golem trembled with rage as he approached, and West felt desperately around in his desk drawer, feeling for a flat, metallic object.

Anton staggered, but righted himself.

West's hand clasped around the device that looked much like a pocket calculator, but infinitely more complex. He desperately punched commands into the keypad. The device began to hum.

Anton made a choking sound, coughed. The sound, however, sounded shockingly like the word, "Why?"

The screen of the device lit up with neon-green

digits. Pseudo-cosmic coordinates.

Anton raised his massive arms –

And West was gone.

The juggernaut smashed his arms down on an empty desk, splintering the thin wood. Anton let out an animal war-shriek that echoed throughout the entire University.

Reverberated through the very fibres of his pseudo-reality.

==

"The pain is almost too much to bear, father."

West was backed into the corner. The feeling of déjà-vu made him sick to his stomach. He reached into his pocket.

"Only one thing has kept me from madness. One thing has kept me from sheer animal insanity," Anton continued. "Do you know what it is, father?"

West's words stuck in his throat. But he knew what Anton meant.

"Vengeance," Anton said.

West silently clicked buttons on the device in his pocket. His stealth, however, was for naught; lighting fast, Anton was upon him, grasping his arm. Giving it a sharp twist, bones broke, and the device flew from the mad doctor's hand. It shattered on the floor.

"For you see, I know why the Old Ones are unable

to kill you."

West began to hyperventilate.

"To end it all, you needed to have your own power turn on you. To have your own creation destroy you."

Tears streamed from West's good eye.

"Please. Please, no..."

"It had to be me. It always had to be me. And that is why, for all these years, you have lived in fear; for somehow *you knew this all along*."

He grabbed West's throat. His oesophagus made a sickening crunching sound.

"Father," Anton whispered. "You were right to fear."

In one, smooth motion, Anton tore West in half.

In a single second, the entire swarm of Byakhee fell to the floor, dead. The Shoggoth growth began to rain in thick flakes from the ceiling.

==

Back in the mall, the other team was doing a fairly decent job of holding back the undead hordes using automatic crossbows and pulse rifles.

Their fortunes increased exponentially when the entire zombie army fell inanimate, slumping to the floor like rag dolls.

"Okay," Zoë said. "What just happened?"

"They did it," Bas said, her smile widening into a

grin. "They really did it!"

The entire group of PwnCon attendees burst into a (this time) well-placed round of applause and cheering.

For good measure, Aphoom put two more rounds into a nearby corpse's skull.

===

Everyone sighed with relief; West's divided body showed no signs of lingering vitality.

Anton slowly turned, a look of rapture on his tortured face. He looked toward Lavinia. The girl's face was stained with tears of sweet sorrow.

The juggernaut raised his fist, extended his thumb.

Slowly, almost as if he were as statue made entirely from dust and sand, he dissolved into a swirling cloud.

"Until the next reality, my friend," Lavinia said, her voice heavy with emotion. "Enjoy a well-earned rest in the faraway fields of unborn dreams."

"You'll see him again, Lav," Carter said.

"I know," Lavinia said, wiping her eyes. "But today, he is a hero."

===

The National Guard was a little late.

Although that wasn't really their fault, given the

whole Ambiguity Barrier and everything.

They secured the area, and PwnCon had to be moved elsewhere. It continued as planned the next day, however, and the entire strange group of Old Ones and characters attended; with the exception of Lovecraft, who was comatose but clearly healing at a satisfactory rate. They even met a few other Old Ones who had heard about the incident and decided to investigate... after the initial fighting was over, of course.

Yes, it was the vacation of a lifetime, and they would never forget it. Especially those who had almost died.

Once the festivities were over, it was decided that they should drive home in Carter's APC, as it would be a bit too hard to explain the still-comatose Lovecraft at the airport.

"We could just say he's drunk," Aphoom suggested.

"I've been called many things, Aphoom," Carter replied. "Derivative isn't one of them."

DID YOU KNOW?!?!?

It has been decided that, after recent events, next year's PwnCon will be held once more in Finley, at the same locations. The convention will utilize the bizarrely altered hotel architecture as its main attraction, billing it as a "haunted tower" with the unofficial title of "the Hug Tower" for reasons unknown.

Many fans are pleased with this development.

XVIII

In Which the Story Reaches its Conclusion

==

THRESHOLD ISLAND, APRIL 20

Lovecraft suddenly woke, taking in a gasping breath. He looked around, making note of his surroundings. They were familiar, but only vaguely; this was the bedroom in his apartment, a room he barely ever used. He untangled the sheets from his legs, sat up to get out of the bed, but was stopped by the sharp pain in his chest.

He looked down to see the delicately wrapped gauze dressing his chest wound.

"Try not to move too much," a voice from the other end of the room said.

Lovecraft looked up; saw Zoë sitting cross-legged on the armchair opposite the bed.

"You might open your wound again. And that would totally ruin the purpose of your little nap."

"How long was I out?"

"Almost a week."

Lovecraft's eyes widened.

"Don't worry, though. Lav and Carter have been keeping a watch for unusual developments, and they haven't come up with anything."

"Where is everybody?"

"In the other room, having waffles."

"They're all here, in my apartment?"

"They've been worried about you, Craft."

She stood, walked over, sat on the bed. Lovecraft indicated the wound dressing.

"Did you do this?"

"Mhmm."

"Thanks."

A silence fell between them.

"When I was kinda dying back there," Lovecraft said finally. "All I could think of was you. Particularly back when we met. You were cold, and confused, and more importantly totally creeped out by me, and I don't think I was helpful at the time."

Zoë laughed.

Lovecraft lifted a hand to caress her face. "You've been through so much, and you've adapted so well. I'm real proud of the way you handled yourself back there, and more than that, you are most definitely the girl of my dreams."

"Even though I'm pregnant with twin fish hybrids?"

"Would it be weird for me to change that 'even though' to an 'especially since'?"

"Not at all."

She kissed him.

"Besides," Lovecraft said, stroking her hair. "How could I not love a girl who likes *The Phantom of the Opera* and *Alien Monster Chainsaw Horror* at the same time?"

They laughed.

==

On the rooftop of the apartment building Natty stood, watching the gathering storm clouds that resonated the amber light of the setting sun.

Cthulhu, who had appeared behind her, noted how much warmer her pale face looked in this light.

"Looks like it's going to be quite the storm," Cthulhu said.

Natty turned toward him, not at all surprised by his sudden appearance.

"Do you believe him?" She asked cryptically.

"What?"

"Do you really believe Lovecraft? I mean, that we're all fake?"

"Natty," Cthulhu said, stepping closer to her. "He never said we fake. Simply because we are the result of a warped imagination, does not make us fake."

She turned back toward the clouds. They were losing their colour, becoming a dark, gunmetal grey.

"I've got an inkling that this isn't over."

"No," Cthulhu said, putting an arm around her waist. "I feel this, too. Something still out there. But here and now, we not worry. Here and now, we have each other."

Cthulhu kissed Natty, and she returned the kiss with passion.

Suddenly, they felt eyes upon them. They broke their embrace.

Standing next to them, wearing a big, goofy grin, was Joey.

"Mr. Cthulhu," he said. "You look happy."

Oddly enough, he was right; for the first time in his life, Cthulhu wore not a skull-like death-stare, but a mask of shockingly human contentment.

===

OLD ONE CITADEL, SUBDIMENSIONAL PSEUDOCOSMIC PARALLAX – DESIGNATION PR-000

The Citadel was usually pretty quiet this time of day. It was a weekend, so most Old Ones were off vacationing in various alternate universes (PR Triple

Zero was incredibly dull, with absolutely no recreational value). Only necessary personnel were present at this time.

An Old One, who bore the appearance of an overtired nineteen-year-old boy, sat at his desk, watching the various gauges that monitored the energy of each pseudo-reality. This Old One, who called himself simply "Morgan," was assigned to universes PR-140 to PR-212 (212 being a very recent establishment). If he detected a spike in energy levels, he would have to make the necessary calls to bring it back into balance.

It was a dreadfully boring job; especially compared to his private pseudo-reality where he lived on the freshly-terraformed moon. Had a beach house on Lake Armstrong.

Yep, probably the most boring job ever, seeing as most events happened outside his assigned range. But that had changed, as of late.

Morgan felt a tap on his shoulder, and turned to see Ana, his assistant. Ana looked like she was thirteen, but was, in reality, much older. They were all much older than they looked.

"What is it, Ana?" Morgan said, trying to rub the bleariness from his eyes.

"I got you the case file on Event 809-B in PR-212," she replied, handing him a thick Manila envelope.

Morgan removed the contents, looked them over.

"'Severe superficial damage, but no casualties sustained,'" he read. "Not bad for that little screw-up."

"I recall that Lovecraft had assistance, sir."

"Of course he did. I sent them."

"But it was Mr. Ward that tipped us off."

"Someone had to make the calls to our people, and who do you think that was?"

"You, sir."

"That's right. But no matter how good they did cleaning this up, I can't let it go. First the guy accidentally builds a PR, then he nearly causes a full-blown Class-X Apocalypse Scenario, then West saunters over and causes 809-B. Disaster follows this kid, and I want to know why."

"Shall I contact an agent to keep an eye on him?"

"No," Morgan said, his eyes sparkling with malicious intent. "I've got a better idea."

SPECIAL THANKS

Firstly, I would like to thank my family. You have all been incredibly tolerant toward my strange writing patterns and constant caffeine-mongering.

Secondly, thanks go out to the late H.P. Lovecraft. Sorry using you characters thus, Mr. Lovecraft.

Thirdly, the readers at FanFiction.net for reading and liking my fanfiction, which served as a starting point for this book.

Fourthly, to my "fantasy think tank": Michael Crichton, Terry Pratchett, Tim Burton, Joss Whedon, Mike J. Nelson, Terry Gilliam, Douglas Adams, Dean Koontz (sorry there was no dog, Mr. Koontz), Neil Gaiman, and the delightfully awful Peter Chimaera.

And sorry to Mr. Bruce Campbell. The Bruce that exists in PR-212 is based on his portrayal in "My Name is Bruce," not reality. You're unprecedentedly groovy, Mr. Campbell!